GREAT GOOGLY MOOGLY!

GREAT GOOGLY MOOGLY!

The Lowcountry Liar's Tales of History & Mystery

BRIAN WANAMAKER McCRÉIGHT

PELICAN PUBLISHING COMPANY
GRETNA 2013

Copyright © 2013
By Brian Wanamaker McCréight
All rights reserved

> The word "Pelican" and the depiction of a pelican are trademarks of Pelican Publishing Company, Inc., and are registered in the U.S. Patent and Trademark Office.

Library of Congress Cataloging-in-Publication Data

McCreight, Brian, 1955-
  Great googly moogly! : the Lowcountry Liar's tales of history and mystery / by Brian Wanamaker McCreight.
    p. cm.
  Includes bibliographical references.
  ISBN 978-1-4556-1782-1 (pbk. : alk. paper) — ISBN 978-1-4556-1805-7 (e-book) 1. Ghosts—South Carolina. 2. Parapsychology—South Carolina—History. 3. Folklore—South Carolina. 4. Tales—South Carolina. 5. South Carolina—Social life and customs—Anecdotes. I. Title.
  BF1472.U6M398 2013
  133.109757—dc23
                                                  2012044286

Printed in the United States of America
Published by Pelican Publishing Company, Inc.
1000 Burmaster Street, Gretna, Louisiana 70053

*For my parents
and my children—
each one a storyteller*

Contents

Foreword		9
Preface (Foretellin')		11

PART I: THE GREAT

Chapter 1	Cross of St. George	15
Chapter 2	In the Shadow of Sherman	23
Chapter 3	Ol' One-Eye Ollie of Folly	35
Chapter 4	The Silverware Civil War	47
Chapter 5	To the Victor Go the Spoils	61

PART II: THE GOOGLY

Chapter 6	The Edisto Crypt	75
Chapter 7	Love Stinks	85
Chapter 8	Mother's Milk	99
Chapter 9	Rx for a Best-Kept Secret	107
Chapter 10	The Return of "Rumpty Rattles"	119
Chapter 11	The Setting of the *Rising Sun*	127

PART III: THE MOOGLY

Chapter 12	A Cure for What Ails You	139
Chapter 13	The Headless Horse Ma'am	145
Chapter 14	The Little White Dog of White Point Gardens	153
Chapter 15	The Long and the Latitude of It	157
Chapter 16	She Loves Me Knot	161
Chapter 17	Who's Up First?	165

Notes	169
Glossary	173
Bibliography	175

Foreword

I use two words to describe history: *hi-story*. The first word is a friendly greeting—*hi*—and how can you not reply in kind? The second word is the essence of all history ever, recorded or not: *story*. We humans are set apart from all other creatures by our love of story, of being able to communicate and appreciate and ruminate on what happened to whom, when, where, and how. The why brings us to fables, creation myths, and religion itself. It is the "story" in *history* that holds our attention and binds us together.

In this collection of stories from the South Carolina Lowcountry, there is history, mystery, and humor. These are tales of the paranormal—ghost stories of various spectral degrees, accounts of incredibly ironic happenstance, and weird coincidences in life that just cannot be made up. What makes them all the more enjoyable is their narration by a great storyteller whom I have often witnessed in the act of telling the tale, my friend Jim Aisle, the Lowcountry Liar.

After I had heard him tell many a tall tale, I thought I had heard it all. Then as summer changed to autumn, and the harvest moon appeared, Jim began telling tales that could curl your straight hair or straighten your curly locks. He says he likes to tell his "ghostories," as he calls them, after dark, when even the shadows have shadows. Sometimes after listening to Jim, I have a tough time falling asleep. I toss and turn in bed, staring into the gloom and awaiting my imagined doom.

Thankfully, that hasn't come yet. I am still here to tell the tale, as Jim might say. So Jim has told the tales, and I have recorded them for you, dear reader.

These are folk tales, of, by, and for the people. Read the tales alone if you dare, or read them aloud with friends. That is best. The stories were fun to write, but they are meant to be heard.

Make sure there are plenty of lights on, though. You never know who—or what—might be looking over your shoulder.

Brian Wanamaker McCréight

Preface (Foretellin')

When characters are speaking in this book, some regional pronunciations have been used, so a glossary is provided. Although it may appear so, the text is not replete with misspellings. We just talk like that down here.

Make no mistake: nothing written here is meant as an impropriety. Nothing barbaric is blurted out, nor are any good manners of the Lowcountry hoi polloi violated. Where I live, this is the conventional use of language. I know, because these are my very words, not only written but spoken at countless public venues across the Palmetto State for the past few decades.

When asked how long have I been telling stories, many times I have stated, "I have been telling tales for over two centuries." That is to say, I have been entertaining audiences of all ages across South Carolina since the late twentieth century into the twenty-first century. And that is no lie.

The Lowcountry Liar

PART I: THE GREAT

CHAPTER 1

Cross of St. George

My friend Jim Aisle the storyteller, known as the Lowcountry Liar, said he stumbled over this unholy ghost story when he was on the road.

You know, sometimes it's best to leave things well enough alone. If you mess with something, it might mess with you worse and make a mighty mess of you. It's been said to let sleeping dogs lie, so I'll tell you a tale as an example. It ain't no lie.

This all happened at the tail end of the War Between the States and continued with equally dire consequences during the time that followed. That would be the era of Reconstruction or, as we say south of the Mason-Dixon Line, "the error of Wreck-construction." Folks still argue about whichever was the first domino to cause the long, loud fallout between the North and the South. Yet for all the noise made about the load of long suffering, maybe not every tile lying on the table has been examined. Allow me to explain.

In the summer of 1860, a man died. So what, you say? Well sir, this particular man I mean had been a slave brought over from Africa's gold coast some forty years earlier. This certain slave had on him the arcane knowledge of roots and herbs and how to mix them. He knew how to *conjure*. He was what you might call a witch doctor, who could do magic, black or white. A foxtail he wore on his belt, as a talisman or totem.

After this slave landed in Charleston, a rich planter bought him and brought him over to a plantation near the Edisto River in the Colleton District. Other slaves there recognized the conjure man's other-world worth, so they gave him due respect. Soon enough, the slaves started going to him for all sorts of tricks of both the healing and hurting kind. They would make requests for white-magic goodness such as love charms, or for protection from black-magic badness such as vexations. A fine line twisting like the letter *s* separates a *cure* from a *curse,* and you best know the difference, or rue the day.

Well sir, when word would come to the root doctor of a need in the neighborhood for his herbs, he would make a house call to set the spirits straight. After a time, he accumulated money enough to buy himself free, and ever after that he went around tending to the un-emancipated population of the area. Sort of like a circuit rider, but using roots for his religion, he became known as Doc Fox.

Doc Fox set up shop by the Edisto River near the hamlet of St. George. A few generations later, the town, laid right at the crossroads of Highways 78 and 15 today, became the seat of Dorchester County. Back before and during the war, when the counties were districts, St. George was a key railway link between the Lowcountry and Peedee regions to the south and east. From there trains headed to the west side of the state and Georgia as well as north to the hub cities of Orangeburg and Columbia. Yes sir, St. George was in a strategic place all right, right in the crosshairs of commerce and commotion.

During the first week in February of 1865, the Yankees invaded South Carolina and threatened to move up the Salkahatchie River, stretching across the west side of Colleton and Barnwell districts. The next week, they tried to take the town of Augusta, near the Savannah River in Edgefield District. By midmonth, that inhumane Union man Sherman and his hate-filled army stood at the Congaree River, in Lexington District, outside the capital city of Columbia—right in the middle of the state, at the center of secession.

The Confederate forces defended against the constantly shifting lines everywhere they could, but the general odds and General Sherman's overwhelming army were mounting against them. The civilians of South Carolina could only watch and wait and worry about which color uniform they might see next—light gray or dark blue. It was a hellish time for everyone, for true. Plenty of folks, whatever the depth of their faith, knelt at the cross to pray for deliverance from danger.

Having such a crucial railroad hub at St. George, Confederate general Beauregard sent a detachment of troops to build up defenses, or otherwise leave impediments for the Yankees. The Southern soldiers did not know where nor when the Yankees might show up, and they did not want to get cut off from the main Confederate army, so they made a mess of the main roadways to slow down the enemy advance. At St. George, they came across a collection of quarry stones meant for the local graveyard, so they scattered the stones in the highways and at the crossroads. The soldiers searched for other sizeable stones to use for the same purpose. One of the rocks they confiscated they should have left resting where they found it. Some things best be let be. Let sleeping dogs lie, you know.

You see, Doc Fox, the conjure man who had died just before the war, had been buried in the style of his African ancestors, with cultural considerations for his status as a root doctor. Few folks knew the precise site of his grave. With him being a sorcerer, it was a special secretive location, and the traditional African burial plot ain't maintained with manicured lawn mowing and fresh-cut flowers. Instead, the grave will be left to overgrow with grass and weeds in an ultimate exercise of natural recycling. A large common rock might be emplaced as a headstone, which may or may not have a name and date etched into it. Such was the case with Doc Fox's resting place, and you best believe that some sort of sign had been crisscrossed on that stone. Any African slave would have recognized such a sight and gone on about his business, avoiding it all. But the Confederates, even if they knew of the particulars of this practice, were in haste to make defensive preparations so did not notice such details. Someone in gray took that unknown headstone and tossed it on one of the roads around St. George.

Then, just to cross things up, the Yankees never did come by St. George. Sherman, a confounding commander, had his strategy mapped out to look like one thing but result in something else. He had his eye on Columbia all the time, and he fixed to run the Rebels across the state. By the end of April, it was all over, first with General Lee surrendering to General Grant at Appomattox up in Virginia, and finally with General Johnston surrendering to

Sherman over the border in North Carolina near Goldsboro.

Back in South Carolina, the Yankees were cocksure of themselves, and the Southerners, soldier and civilian alike, were too downcast for comment. The slaves, or by now, ex-slaves, were *pure-tee* jubilant. In all the upheaval and hullabaloo, nobody gave a hoot about some hole in the ground in a small town. With all the hubbub of the war, there were plenty of holes in the ground, all sorts of depressions.

With the headstone gone off the grave like a cork off a bottle, the spirit of Doc Fox the conjure man was let out. His spirit flowed out like whiskey to intoxicate the local populace. Ironic, ain't it, how whiskey's called "the water of life" as well as "firewater." But then, alcohol can be either a tonic or a toxin, both a *cure* and a *curse*. It depends on saturation.

Well sir, that spirit of Doc Fox surely did saturate the land and the folks living there with bad luck. As if the war had not been bad enough, more torment came to South Carolina: martial law, occupation by Federal forces, political-party shenanigans by the ruling righteous Republicans versus the demonizing Democrats, and everywhere heartbreaking, abject poverty. An almost tangible tickling ran across everyone's shoulders, as if something unholy and wholly unknown and unwelcome was about to descend upon them. Drought struck St. George, and stuck for years. The farmlands had already been despoiled by soldiers. Now the days were hot and dusty, yet the nights were humid and clammy. The only moisture was in the air. The nearby Edisto River dropped in volume; some local creeks dried up completely. The riverbanks held deposits of rocks, fallen timber, and sundry debris.

What crops grew fared poorly. The cotton kept a yellow pallor. Melons and beans were puny in size and yield. Greens barely qualified in namesake, they were so pallid. The corn yielded small cobs. Even the white lightning made from the corn mash seemed mighty short of the spark, and right at a time when a drink was sorely needed, too.

The cows gave sour milk, those that gave any, and their moos sounded more like moans. Farmyards were half-full of scrawny chickens—some paltry poultry, yes sir. Even the pigs could not keep any weight on, and folks were evermore aching for bacon. Most all the horses became swaybacked or spavined, and the hair fell out of their manes and tails. That could have been from overwork, sure, but every horse around whinnied with a worry and neighed too nervously, as though they could sense something unseen by humankind. When the pigs rooted and grunted, it sounded like people muttering something in secret—something awful, like some kind of incantation.

Only the goats fattened up and procreated well, which many folks saw as the Devil's doing. Even so, they put the goats to good work, milking them or hitching them to little wagons and carts. Goat carts got to be real popular in the Lowcountry, even in the urbane city of Charleston, where goat carts—not go-carts— appeared in a famous storybook and a grand ol' opry, too—that being *Porgy* and then *Porgy and Bess*.[1] But the summertime wasn't so easy back then.

Anyway, as popular as the goats got to be, another animal became equally unpopular: foxes. They began overrunning the countryside. The invaders multiplied, eating up the scrawny yard birds, digging up crop roots, barking at night like the wild dogs they are, and generally terrorizing the black and white populace alike. Like the *scalawag and carpetbagger* vermin who were spoiling the local economy, the foxes were living off the hard-luck toil of others, with no end in sight.

After several years of this distress, the folks around St. George called a meeting to address the mess. In the course of the conversing, someone solemnly spoke the word *"mojo,"* and then someone mentioned ol' Doc Fox, and that caused a long silence. It seemed as if the hex was in. Finally there was a unanimous vote to search for the grave of ol' Doc Fox and make sure his headstone was in its proper place. Folks had to rest assured that their location in life was not overly affected by the population of the afterlife. They figured that if what you don't know won't hurt you, then what you know you don't know could come and get you.

For weeks, months, and years after that, folks scoured the St. George area to find where Doc Fox the conjure man lay. Often a hole or mound was discovered, and the word went round, but it would prove to be only a natural occurrence. Plenty of rocks were rooted up, but none seemed right fitting for Doc Fox, and none had markings on it for him.

For more than a decade after the war, during the sordid stretch of time of Reconstruction, the folks of St. George searched for Doc Fox's remains. Some folks gave up, yet lived in dread. Some quit to move out West, and who knows what fate befell them out on the prairie or in the desert. Still others kept at it, looking every which-a-wheres, till finally the Federal occupiers left, and then, lo and behold, they found the remains of Doc Fox.

It was too obvious, right under their noses. One day while conducting a survey before widening the highways, a work crew came across an odd depression at the east side of the town's crossroads. At first they thought it was some water ditch. Then they saw a bone. Then they found the tail of a fox in the hole, and they stopped searching. Everyone knew then that Doc Fox lay buried at that crossroads. The whole time they had been looking for him, the little town of St. George had grown up right at his feet.

His headstone showed up a few blocks away soon after, at the Blessed Redeemer Baptist Church of all places. It turned out to be a nondescript rock that the sexton had used as a simple doorstop outside the church vestibule. Nobody had noticed the rock much before, but on the first Sunday following the finding of the remains, during the first rain in some time, somehow the rock rolled away from the door. The rock lay upturned in the lot, rain washed to reveal scratches on its flat face that spelled out:

DOC
FOX
MD
CCC
LX

Well sir, by the following Friday, a cortege was formed by folks who on the one hand were greatly relieved to have found the remains of Doc Fox while on the other hand were supremely saddened all the same. They mourned for both the past and the present. For the future they kept hope and kept hoping, and they kept a secret.

The big secret they kept was and still is where they relocated Doc Fox. It was out of town, obviously—most likely down by the banks of the Edisto River, looking back to Africa to the east. A man has got to lie down near the water, for its constant movement and its property for sustaining life. That much everyone knows, but what ain't known is the map coordinates for how to find Doc Fox. He is good and buried.

Once Doc Fox was relocated, the folks of St. George noticed that all the odd and unlikely goings on stopped going on. Life there ain't never been perfect, but where is such a place in the first place? Folks in St. George don't feel no heavy hex around their necks the way they did when ol' Doc Fox had been let loose.

Nowadays when you look at a map of South Carolina, make special note of an area where the county lines meet at a crossroads. The Edisto River marks the division between Orangeburg and Bamberg counties as well as between Colleton and Dorchester counties. The state government bisected the county lines on the Edisto at Highway 21, running due north and south.

Folks say that somewhere in the vicinity of that four-county junction, near the banks of the Edisto River, lie the mortal, or maybe immortal, remains of Doc Fox. Go look for yourself. Only, if you should happen to find ol' Doc Fox's headstone rock in an out-of-the-way spot, all overgrown and bramble-bush hidden, well sir, do the universe and all us in it a favor, please. Don't mess with the rock or what's beneath it! Let things lie where they lie, the way they lie. Nobody wants to rouse up any residual magic that is resting in the ground, now, do they?

It's said that Robert Johnson, the great blues guitar player, sold his soul to the Devil at a crossroads. Could it happen to you, too? Be careful when you look into the past, because something may come back to bite you. Remember, as Brer Rabbit would say: *"Don't never trouble Trouble till Trouble troubles you!"*

I asked Jim to show me on a map the approximate burial spot of Doc Fox.
"Why?" Jim asked me.
I replied, "So I can avoid it."

CHAPTER 2

In the Shadow of Sherman

One New Year's Eve, the Lowcountry Liar told me this tale as an anniversary observance of a ghostly occurrence.

Martin Macbeth, like his Confederate contemporary John Wilkes Booth, was a thespian, a professionally trained actor performing the plays of Shakespeare, be they tragedy, comedy, or history. Before the sordid War Between the States, in theaters North and South, Martin often portrayed the doomed Scottish king who was his namesake. But by late 1864, the war upstaged everything, and it seemed to Martin that no one on either side remembered his footlight fame.

So hit by hard luck, as though he had been on the receiving end of a cannonball, Martin Macbeth became nearly destitute on account of the war. As difficult as it is to earn a living as an artist of any kind at any time, it got to be downright next to impossible to exist as an actor while events such as the Battle of Gettysburg got all the press. Now, on the one hand, folks need artistic distractions from the daily news of destruction and mayhem. On the other hand, real-life dramas sometimes get to be too distracting for folks to appreciate any artistic endeavors.

Perhaps in part, Martin Macbeth's bad luck had to do with his surname and its association with that hapless Scottish king. Actors can be super superstitious. They still refer to Willy the Spear-shaker's tragedy of *Macbeth* as "the Scottish play." They never utter the name in a theater, for fear of invoking the wrath of some wraith on stage. A well-known whisper in the theater has it that an actor once tempted Fate and spoke the name of that play before his entrance, then went on and died on stage—literally. It was not because of his performance. He died on stage because his heart stopped and he quit breathing, for true. There could be a curse on the name after all.

Down in Charleston, the so-called hotbed of secession, one of Martin's distant cousins, Charles Macbeth, served as the city's mayor during the war. That is some luck. Like I say, there could be a curse on the name. By the end of 1864, it wasn't that much to be mayor of—most of downtown Charleston was deserted. From Calhoun Street down to White Point Gardens and cutting across the peninsula, the port city had became a ghost town.

The desertion resulted from Federal shelling. The Feds commenced the fiendish fireworks in the summer of 1863 and did not stop until after Valentine's Day in 1865. They shot some twenty-six thousand shells. The Yankees used church steeples as targets, even on Sundays! Is there any wonder why we say "damn Yankees"?

Well sir, Charleston is known for its long tradition of religious tolerance and its great variety of worship houses, so it is called the "Holy City," but during the bombardment, the lower part of town became a "Holey City." Practically every building down there got hit; some structures were flat-out destroyed. It didn't matter whether the building was a church, hospital, business, or home. For over a year and a half, the Yankees kept it up, making the bombardment of Charleston the longest terror attack on civilians anywhere in these United States. It takes a special kind of government employee for that—uncivil.

However, Charleston never did surrender. That's a mistaken assumption made by some, not accounting for gumption. The only time we surrendered was back in 1780 when an entire Continental army got trapped by the British army and navy. It was the greatest British victory during the Revolution. The American general who did the surrendering was a Massachusetts man by name of Benjamin *Lincoln*—I kid you not. Now that's what you call foreshadowing.

Sad Martin Macbeth left Richmond, Virginia with only the spirit of bad luck to keep him company as he zigzagged away from the war. Once he got to Charleston to visit his cousin the mayor, Martin expected to turn things around for himself somehow. At the very least, he hoped to celebrate Christmas with his relatives.

The Yuletide holiday of 1864 in the Lowcountry wasn't too merry, though. Come Christmas Day, the Yankees celebrated the birthday of Christ by firing 200 rounds of unbrotherly love into Charleston. Throughout the city, pieces of brick, timber, and shrapnel fell like confetti. It was hardly a celebration.

Martin missed out on the shebang, arriving two days after Christmas. With the tracks still out of range of the Yankee guns, the trains were running, but Martin was too down on his luck to be able to afford a fare. Heck, his luck was down on *him*.

Luck was low in Charleston too, with destroyed buildings and debris-filled streets. It took Martin another two days to locate his cousin Charles. The mayor was glad to renew the family acquaintance, though there was nothing he could do for Martin except tell him to duck for cover. He did invite Martin to his New Year's Eve party to ring in what everyone hoped would be a better future. Martin decided to stay for the party, but he didn't know where he might go or even what he might do after that.

The last day of 1864 dawned with overcast skies, gray as a Confederate uniform. The Yankees continued bombarding the city, promising nothing new to anyone. Nonetheless, by nightfall, candle-lighting time, Charlestonians were ready to celebrate the change in the calendar.

At eight o'clock, Mayor Macbeth's New Year's Eve party got started. The mayor introduced his cousin in a general address to the crowd. Martin mingled with the guests, danced with the ladies, joked with the men, recited Shakespeare to everyone's delight, and had a grand time. From across the harbor, the Yankees fired blanks to shout out the old year, acknowledging the annual change. After having endured so much Northern noise for so long, no one in town took a mind to them.

The nine o'clock chimes were hardly noticed by the revelers.

In what seemed like a minute, the ten o'clock hour chimed in.

A quick tick later, eleven o'clock passed by.

The final minutes marched on to midnight as if the old year couldn't wait to retire.

Martin, like the other guests, lost sense of the time while he socialized. Enjoying the high life, he also lost track of the number of toasts he drank. A long list of liquid salutes honored all the members of the Confederate cabinet as well as every valiant Southern general, be he alive or dead. Then, as true Charlestonians, everyone turned undivided attention to Charleston. Toasts to the town, what was left of it, had no one feeling at all melancholy but made everybody the merrier as midnight neared.

The clocks kept clicking till the hands stood straight up, finally chiming twelve times. Then followed shouts of jubilation, pistols fired in the general direction of the Federal batteries, and kisses all round. Great joy for a hopeful future was shared by one and all, even by Martin Macbeth. The potential for good luck stirred the mix of well-wishing, glad-handing, back-slapping glee.

Martin, feeling highly spirited from the imbibed spirits, wandered off shortly after this stage of the celebrations. He felt emboldened to explore the bombed-out part of town. So, arming himself with a bottle of blockade-run champagne, and bearing a candlestick and taper like a lit banner, Martin marched off to meet whatever enemy he imagined to be roaming amongst the ruins of Charleston.

You know, in the magical, early hours of a new year, with or without alcohol, you can find yourself in strange surroundings or situations, and you will probably survive to tell the tale. But to be inebriated and alone in the middle of the night, while amongst the ruins of a military target during a war, that ain't like nothing scripted by any omnipresent playwright. Who knows from whom Martin was taking direction. There ain't no clue as to where he got his cue to do what he did. Maybe it was just the bubbly bubbling over.

The ghastly remains of bombarded buildings loomed like towering tombstones as Martin made his way through the ruins. Moonlight disappeared and reappeared as silent clouds slid across the blackened sky. The Yankee cannons slept, the quiet of the night disturbed only by occasional punctuations of distant potshots and Rebel yells.

Between midnight and daybreak, the hags and *haints* prowl and howl. It's the time of night when mysterious creatures with unblinking *plat eyes* stare at you from the shadows or just suddenly appear, ill defined, in your path. You might scream. Well, you might try but make no sound. But you won't never forget what you've just seen.

Brave Martin Macbeth was drunk enough to be oblivious to the faint night sounds and the eerie surroundings as he soldiered on. He was only mindful of his own murky purpose. He headed towards the end of the peninsula, across from the mouth of the harbor, where he could look out to Fort Sumter guarding Charleston from the Federal navy. He planned to propose his own toasts to the stubborn defenders of the port city, to proudly proclaim his own respectful thanks to those stalwart souls who bravely bore up daily under enemy fire and returned it in kind. Perhaps the sundry spirits of the night moved Martin in his patriotism to throw up his heartfelt salutes. Perhaps the spiritual influence of firewater worked its wonder, too. *In vino veritas,* they say.

A soft, salt-flavored breeze blew around Martin as he looked out over the *Bat-tree* wall to behold the expanse of cold, black water of the harbor. He set down the candle, uncorked the bottle, and faced the darkness over the water. In turn, Martin addressed each of the five forts ringing the harbor, thanking the defenders for their daily display of bravery, and with each thanks he gulped down a mouthful of champagne.[1] Then turning about face, Martin praised the Holy City for the steadfast resistance of her citizens, as well as her romantic charm, or what was left of it.

The bottle was nearly empty. Martin stared at the contents, measuring the remaining good spirits with a gleeful grin. He realized then that liquid reinforcements stood ready at the party back uptown. So picking up the candlestick and again holding it aloft, he began the return trek for refreshments.

He didn't get too far. Instead of heading northward, Martin mistakenly meandered from east to west to east again, finally stopping only a block from where he had made his toasts. And being so unsure of his bearings, he slowly became unsure of his bravery in the situation. To strengthen his courage, Martin took another swig from the bottle.

He gazed up at the stars and hazily determined that north was just around the corner. He wobbled down a street and at the next corner turned left onto Zigzag Alley, a deadend dogleg road.[2] Weaving down the zig and following along the zag, he reached the end of the alley at a tall, dark wall.

Martin panicked. He looked up and down the wall, but no threshold could be seen. He turned round quickly, making himself dizzy and nearly falling down.

In a moment, the spinning stopped and Martin felt more clearheaded, perhaps from the adrenaline racing through his veins. He noticed the candle getting short, uncomfortably short, soon to be only a puddle of wax. Acknowledging he was lost, and alone, and drunk in the dead of night, he realized too that his only weapon was the knife in his boot. His only other ally was the courage in the bottle—what was left of it.

Without another thought, Martin stumbled to the rubble of the nearest wrecked house. He figured it would be better to spend the night in some sort of safe haven and wrap himself in a blanket of wine. The night hours would only get colder and he wasn't getting any bolder, so in he went.

Most of the roof was ruined, and an entire wall was gone, but Martin found himself a cozy corner in a small hallway behind the main staircase. He sat against the wall, curled up close as a cat, and tried to relax. He nearly drifted off to sleep when he heard something, or someone, nearby.

Martin held up the candle, looking for a rat, but no, it wasn't a scurrying sound. It was more like slow steps. Then it stopped. Martin set the candle down and tried to get comfortable again. The steps resumed, coming closer. Martin reached for the knife in his boot, preparing to spring up.

In a blink, a man stood before him: a big fellow, but kind of faded looking. Maybe it was the shadows, but the man appeared to have no color in his face. Maybe he'd been sick, or worn down by the elements. He looked kind of ghostly.

Martin stared up at the big man, not sure if he be friend or foe. Neither of them moved till, swallowing hard, Martin found his professional stage voice. "Who are you, sir?" he demanded. "What do you want?"

The man didn't speak. He didn't blink. He just stared down at Martin with dark plat eyes, like a raccoon caught in the beam of a flashlight during a nighttime backyard visit.

"I have no valuables, sir," offered Martin.

That didn't sway the man. Martin tightened his grip on his knife, waiting. The few seconds seemed like hours.

Finally, the man spoke. "Wait," he said in a low, raspy voice. "Wait." That's all he said. Then he folded his arms over his chest and spread his legs apart, making it evident that neither he nor Martin would be leaving anytime soon.

Looking the strange man up and down, Martin could see he was no match against this fellow's bigness. Then Martin noticed how the man's attire looked kind of old-fashioned, from maybe two centuries ago. He looked like a pirate, like old Blackbeard himself. He wore buckled shoes, ratty stockings, knee-length pants, a long calico overcoat, a stained blouse beneath, a dark scarf tied round his throat, and a broad-brimmed hat with a fluffy feather stuck in it. Across his chest he had slung a wide leather belt with holsters for a pair of percussion pistols, not revolvers. A cutlass hung at his hip. He might have been a colorful pirate, only he had no color, just grayness all over his body.

Who was he? Martin wondered. The question displaced his fear slightly, but still he felt uncomfortable with the situation. Just comparing details like that cutlass to his little blade was enough to convince Martin to stay put.

Pondering his predicament, Martin heard a new sound. It came from overhead, descending the staircase—a swishing sound. It got louder as whatever, or whoever, it was passed above him. He noted that no boards creaked on the stairs, so it had to be a lightweight, surefooted walker.

The pirate stepped aside as a pale woman appeared before Martin. She curtsied, and Martin reluctantly nodded back. She said nothing, though, and in the pause Martin noticed that her clothing came from maybe a century before, the Colonial era. She wore a moll cap, a linen apron, and a floor-sweeping striped dress, not a bustle or hoop skirt, with the ends of a tattered petticoat peeking out beneath. Just like a picture of old Molly Pitcher, Martin thought, only this woman seemed as gray as the pirate.

"Who, who are you, ma'am, if you might allow so bold a question?" he asked her.

She made no reply. An eternal moment passed. Martin tried not to stare at her. She also had unblinking plat eyes, so shiny, but without depth. Martin started to speak again when her mouth opened. Martin thought she would address him, but instead, she turned to the pirate.

"Wait," said the pirate. "Wait."

The pale woman turned back to Martin and said, "Wait."

"Wait?" asked Martin. "Wait for what? Or who? Who are we waiting for?"

"Wait," repeated the pale woman. She said no more than that.

Martin started to get up. The pirate took a step towards him and Martin stopped, crouching halfway up. Slowly he slid down against the wall and sat back on the floor.

He felt for the bottle and held it up to measure the contents. He pulled out the cork with a wet *pop* and touched the open bottleneck to his lips. The pale woman let out a loud sigh and shook her head.

Disgust? Martin wondered. Well, be disgusted, then. Y'all are spooking me.

He tilted his head back, but before he could drink, the pirate reached out and snatched the bottle out of his hand. Then, the pirate upturned the bottle and drank down the dregs. Martin sat in shock, his eyes wide, but said nothing as the champagne disappeared.

The pirate released the bottle, letting it smash to pieces as it hit the floor. The loud crash made Martin jump. He sat looking at the mess of glass, at a loss for words.

Then Martin heard a dripping sound. He looked up expecting to find a leak but could find no water source. Then he looked back at the pair of spooky companions. Champagne dripped from between the pirate's fingers held over his belly, and he was evermore smiling a gruesome gap-toothed grin. The pale woman pursed her lips.

Martin's mouth fell open. "What the—"

"Wait," said the pirate, just a-grinning.

"What did you do?"

"Wait," the pale woman said.

"But—"

"Wait," called out a deep voice.

Martin caught his breath. It was a new voice, someone unseen. Who?

The pirate and the woman stepped back as a dusty black man drifted down the crowded hallway. Looking just as faded as the other two visitors, this man was dressed in attire of maybe a half-century ago. He wore no overcoat, only a paisley waistcoat, with a ruffled shirt, big bowtie, long trousers, and boots. A house slave? wondered Martin. A freedman? No doubt it was another old soul of historic Charleston, but who?

Martin didn't know what to think. However drunk he had been, he was sobering up right quick. That was about all he could do at the moment. He knew trouble well enough when he saw it, and these three looked like trouble, for true. They looked like haints.

None of them spoke; they just stood there blocking Martin's escape. The pirate held his fingers over his dripping belly, grinning all devilish. The pale woman set her hands on her hips, frowning at Martin as though she smelled something *kee-yarn*—deader than dead. The dusty black man leaned against the staircase, drumming his fingers on a step—*drrrummmm, drrrummmm, drrrummmm.*

Then Martin heard someone faintly whistling "Dixie." Martin's felt a little relief, a little emboldened. Reinforcements were coming at last. A-men.

But no. The three haints shifted closer. A Confederate soldier appeared. He was all gray, naturally, but he seemed to be gray through and through—clothes and skin. He was gray as Spanish moss.

Martin didn't wait for pleasantries. "Who are you?"

The soldier smiled at him. Suddenly, he sprang to attention and saluted. Then he turned to the dusty man, who turned to the pale woman, who turned to the pirate.

"Wait," said the dripping pirate, grinning at Martin.

"Wait," said the angry pale woman, turning to stare a hole through Martin.

"Wait," said the dusty black man, turning to wink at Martin.

"Wait," said the soldier, back at attention. "Wait, Martin. Wait."

"Wait!" exclaimed Martin. "That all y'all can say? Wait? What in hell we waiting for?"

"Wait," the soldier repeated. "Wait, Martin. *Wait till Sherman comes!*"

The specters echoed him. *"Wait till Sherman comes! Wait till Sherman comes!"*

The Confederate soldier started to fade away. Then he began breaking up into tiny pieces. "See you in Secessionville,"[3] he said before disappearing.

Martin's eyes went wide. His mouth formed a little "oh." He didn't dare move.

The dusty man half-bowed, came back up, and lifted his hand, as if to bid farewell. Instead, he grabbed the top of his head and pulled it clean off his shoulders. "I got hung and swung from the freedom tree with Denmark Vesey!" he cried, his dusty self crumbling into ashes . . . and then he was gone.

The pale woman cackled like a hag, grabbed her skirts, and pulled them up to show she had no legs beneath—no stockings and no shoes. "My reward from the British!" she hissed. "They chained me up in a prison ship for six months. Gangrene!" She began fading away, cackling all the while, until there was silence.

The pirate laughed a God-awful guffaw. He threw his hands out from his belly to reveal a huge hole where his midsection should have been. "Cannonball!" he bellowed . . . and laughing, he too disappeared.

Martin's heart beat hard and fast. He couldn't swallow. He drew in breaths like a drowning man. Then once more he heard the chorus, "Wait. Wait, Martin, wait. *Wait till Sherman comes!*"

Martin found his voice. "Wait, like hell! Tell Sherman I ain't waiting!"

Martin jumped up, ran out of the house, and skedaddled to the deadend wall. He leaped, grabbed the top of the wall, and landed on the other side. Spirits of one kind or another must have inspired his superhuman effort. The streets lay still, deserted as a graveyard. Martin ran.

No one's seen hide nor hair of Martin Macbeth since.

It could be he traveled westwards. If so, he might have made a new name for himself on the San Francisco stage. He might have sworn off drinking too. Who knows.

I guess all them haints that Martin saw that New Year's Eve of 1864-into-5 came to warn him of a dire future for Charleston, should he wait to see for himself. The funny thing is, Sherman never did come to the Holy City to end the war. He felt that the people already were too dispirited. So much for such things that go bump in the night.

I stared at Jim. All he said was, "Boo!"

Note

This old tale is known under several names and usually includes a series of ever larger, creepy cats intoning the warning. Jim replaced the spooky cats with several spirits representing the diverse history of Charleston. Over the centuries, we've had marauding pirates like Blackbeard, slave uprisings like that of Denmark Vesey, and the American Revolution and the Civil War, both with siege and occupation. (Vesey bought his freedom with his winnings from a New Year's Day lottery in Charleston, lived as a free black carpenter, then led an unsuccessful slave rebellion in 1822; he was hanged for his troubles.) That is all in addition to the citywide fires, floods, earthquakes, hurricanes, and deadly epidemics. Nevertheless, a true native considers Charleston a paradise. That's a paradox. That's Charleston.

Ironically, much of the city had been destroyed by a massive fire a year after secession. The ruins of the lower peninsula are the setting for this ghost story. Sherman did not attack Charleston but had lived there for several years in the 1840s when stationed at Fort Moultrie on Sullivan's Island.

CHAPTER 3

Ol' One-Eye Ollie of Folly

The Lowcountry Liar was crabbing along the rock groins of Folly Beach when he fished up this tale about an erstwhile history-making island resident.

The South has won fame, or infamy, as a haven for a wide variety of colorful characters who amuse and bemuse the rest of us, Southerner or not. The adventures of some of these odd Southern folks—such as Brer Rabbit, Lil Abner, Scarlett O'Hara, to name a few—have been well documented. Yet, other eccentric characters from Dixie ain't as well known outside the South, and they've become some of the South's best-kept secrets.

No doubt, a large measure of the so-called Southern eccentricity comes from perceptions and allegations by foreign folks, who also have superstitious views that they project on us. Nonetheless, some of that Southern eccentricity derives exclusively from vocal locals, rural residents or urban citizens, who believe deeply in the intangible. Down South, the ethereal is often easily shared as an informal faith, held as a profound belief in a spirit world of haints, boo hags, plat eyes, and other things that go bump in the night—things not made by design or mankind but by the mind. Believing is seeing, seeing is believing, and the rest, we call history.

Sometimes you hear someone down South swear they would exchange any number of eyeteeth for something they highly covet. The eyeteeth, you know, are the four pointy canines, the gripping and tearing teeth, that line up below your eyes. You may someday feel that you want to swap these uppers and lowers for whatever thing else you value just as much. You have got to really, really, really want it for that kind of discomfort and disfigurement.

You might be tempted to gamble away all your mouth bones

in order to have more than enough money, or to own a wealth of possessions, or to attain some social position. Having such a doggone strong urge, maybe risking your very life for something, is a fitting definition of *desire*.

Let me tell you a tale of desire, from back during the War of Northern Aggression, or the War for Southern Independence, whichever side of the fence you see it from. It happened when the Yankees were highly anxious, downright desirous, to capture Charleston, the so-called hotbed of secession. In the spring of 1862, the Union army began landing on the beaches of several barrier islands near Beaufort. As we say with a smile, the Yankees came to Hilton Head Island back then and they ain't left yet. The Union army worked its way up the coast, till they came close to Folly Island, just outside Charleston harbor. The Yankee attempts at capturing this valuable port city, positioned on a peninsula between the Ashley and Cooper rivers, had been repeatedly repulsed. The city was sufficiently protected from attack by a ring of fire from five forts surrounding the harbor.

Barrier islands such as Folly became buffers between the ocean and solid mainland, a real no-man's land. A slew of slaves had congregated on Folly, in expectation of freedom. But it all was folly, because the Yankees quickly rounded them up and shipped them down to Hilton Head Island to press them into menial servitude for the many well-heeled Northern officers. No other civilians lived on Folly, as anyone with sense enough had left the sand dunes to the seagulls when the Yankees arrived. That was in the historic records, anyway. You know, it's said that history gets written by the victors. It's also said that the losers know the truth.

I know a local account of one unaccounted-for old soul who sat out the war on the island of Folly. This lone denizen was a woman, of unknown age but spry and quite capable. She'd been living on Folly Island for many years, some say since the second war with England back in 1812. She kept to herself; no one even knew her name for sure. However, it was generally agreed that she was called Laurel Oliver.

Perhaps her penchant for solitude came from her particular

personality. Folks said her demeanor measured somewhere on a mercurial scale between taciturn and cantankerous. Like a bad-tempered turtle, she had a hard plate exterior and a crusty disposition. Besides her irascibility, she was identifiable by the shiny, solid-gold triangular tooth that sat in place of her upper left eyetooth. It was obvious when she spoke, or grimaced a ragged smile. That surely was an eyecatcher, and a sight better than a black hole in the gum line. For that, everyone calls her "Ol' One-Eye Ollie."

Folks speculated on how Ol' One-Eye Ollie, living like a hermit on a barrier island, could afford a solid-gold eyetooth, but no one knew when she first came to Folly, so no one could vouchsafe any claims. No one ever accused her of being a thief, or something worse, like a grave-robbing body snatcher. Some supposed she came across some flotsam or jetsam from a boat wreck. Others swore she had uncovered a cache of pirate loot buried on Folly Beach. They said she still had a king's ransom stashed away somewhere, probably under her hut. But that's all gossip of the idle, since nobody ever found any gold like that out there, and anyway, everyone steered clear of Ollie's homemade hut, mainly because they couldn't find it.

She located her hut halfway up the island by the Folly River, on the lee side, the north side, and ain't that ironic? Lee on the North side! Well, Ol' Ollie's hut sat atop a hillock, like a little folly all its own, but hidden from view by oleander bushes and crepe myrtle trees. Ol' Ollie's snug little shanty by the sea was secret, secure, yet a known landmark, if only you knew where to look.

Halfway through the war, in April 1863, the Yankees arrived at the lower end of Folly Island—it runs southwest to northeast. Then as now, that lower end is mostly uninhabitable, exposed to the wind and tides, a barren spot that not even a gator would favor. That's where the Yankees landed, adding some sixty regiments—nearly thirty thousand troops—over the course of the war. The bluecoats overran the island like sand crabs, and in the process they dug up the landscape, consuming the natural resources.

Ol' Ollie they left alone, but after all, her hut lay hidden in plain sight a good distance from the Yankee landing. Come summertime, the oleanders and crepe myrtles, bushy with green leaves, bloomed with clusters of white and pink flower. Such an array of attractive colors served as contrast to the death and destruction of the war.

Keeping an eye on things, the Yankees kept pickets around the perimeter while crews down at the docks unloaded the Union fleet. Besides the initial invasion and occupation, picket duty and unpacking was all the action on Folly Island ever officially recorded by the United States Army. Those boys in blue—dark-blue flannel—would be left solo with the boring chore of picket duty, standing for hours shouldering a loaded rifle with bayonet in the high heat and heavy humidity of the Lowcountry. The soldiers also had a special company in their companies, a variety of vermin from gnats to rats that always invade with an army. On Folly, the no-see-em-bit-me bugs such as fleas, flies, and mosquitoes were incessantly buzzing round and bothering the blue bodies. That dark Yankee blue must have been an attractive color to such pests. For most all them Northern soldiers, little Folly Island became a place unfit for human habitation, an island aptly named for anyone who ever attempted to occupy it.

Yet for a solitary soul the likes of Ol' Ollie, Folly was just fine—nothing finer in Carolina. She would inhale the aroma of the *pluff mud,* listen to the constant song of the ocean, and witness the violet and blue hues in the Carolina sky. For Ollie, every moment of the day came by like a slow smile, and every day had a happy ending. Come candle-lighting time, between sunset and the first twinkling star of night, Ol' Ollie would retire to her hut.

Sitting in her rocking chair, Ollie would work by candlelight repairing fish or crab nets, mending clothes, or knitting a bed cover. She had no need for a newspaper, even with the war happening right nearby. She'd grown used to the solitude of the island, a secret unto itself.

Ollie followed the same regimen every evening. After giving a yawn (which she got to calling her "li'l visitors") and a stretch once, twice, three times, she'd have a snack, cutting off a mouthful of her latest seaside catch, which she kept hanging high and dry from a hook near the fireplace. She might nibble on flounder or sea trout, but her favorite fish by far was fried red drum, the spot-tail bass.

Then she would go to bed. Yes sir, that was the way to end the day for Ol' Ollie: lying abed while chewing a chunk of fried, dried, wall-hung, spot-tail bass.

Now, some folks might speculate that Ol' Ollie was up to no good in the dark of night out at her hidden hut. Whispers heard around the Lowcountry of boo hags and raw bloody bones might also refer to her. Part of that was the gossip about the golden treasure supposedly hidden under Ollie's hut. The Yankees got wind of the tale, though nothing official ever was done to investigate. They were too busy trying to kill Confederates and capture Charleston.

As any soldier knew then, and knows good and well now too, the fortunes of war can come or go, so a soldier need grab whatever he might find and hold on for dear life. Too many of them Yankee troops seemed to be especially well suited for the stabbing and grabbing duty. These "bummers," as we called them, would confiscate anything of value not moving, and if it moved, it often got shot. Some bummers got so desperate, without regard for their uniform, or perhaps because of it, that they organized secret stealing squads. Generally it was done with a nod and a wink from the Federal authorities, so long as the chain of command also received a percentage of the take. So be it still today, the so-called honor among thieves.

Many men in that Yankee army for sure had heard of Ollie's hidden treasure, and who knows how many truly believed in its existence . Three particular soldiers got tempted beyond redemption to try to find out the truth about Ollie's alleged good fortune. Maybe the heat, humidity, pests, disease, and war increased their desire to know. These three gullible and greedy soldiers would deign to destroy Ollie's solitude for a fortune, so deep was the desire.

None of these three malingering misfits was first-line personnel; they all worked the supply lines, from the backside of the battlefield. They'd been involved in lucrative black-market trade from every coastal loading dock since landing in Beaufort. They otherwise ducked out of any arduous army duty, making this little squad what's known as "gold bricks." They were a menace among menacing men, an unavoidable consequence of war.

One of the three, a sergeant of the 100th New York Volunteers by name of Drummond, was called "Barbarosa" for his full red beard. He was a big, burly fella so he commanded authority. Barbarosa had a deep scar across his right eye from shrapnel caught at Shiloh the year before, leaving him half-blind.[1] He had the appearance of a salty-dog pirate; he could have been the notorious Blackbeard's own red-headed stepson.

His enterprising cohort was a private of the 100th, a ferret-faced fellow who didn't look old enough to shave but had the makings of a goatee shading his chin. His name was something like Gracy or maybe "greasy," because he was a slippery customer for true, with larceny in his eye and ever watchful for an opportunity to exploit an unsuspecting victim. He shipped out from Belfast, Ireland, suspected of burglary and fraud, and upon landing in New York City lined up to muster into Mr. Lincoln's army.

The third member of this misfit outfit was a Corporal Smalls, called "Stump-Foot Charlie." A few weeks earlier, he had lost two toes off his right foot while playing a drunken game of mumbly peg barefoot. He lost the game too, but the mishap got him out of guard duty for a while. He served with the Second South Carolina Colored Infantry, a volunteer unit made up of ex-slaves from the area. What he knew about Lowcountry lore the other two knew about the craft of graft. Now as auxiliary auxiliaries, working the supply docks, these three supplied their criminal cronies with whatever the government issued.

The three liberators took the liberty of making forays into farmyards to requisition livestock or pick up anything they considered Confederate contraband, which made for a considerable list. They bartered these ill-gotten gains among the bluecoats, enlisted and officer alike. Even though business was business, these nefarious thieves only wound up encouraging everyone else to distrust them. They might have been able to keep the officer corps in eggs, but they would never be invited to sit at the same table, regardless of rank. They were another kettle of fish, for true. They would soon be fish in deep hot water, too.

Now, as far as fish and fishing went, Folly Island was a fine spot for any angler. On one hot August day, when the sun lay over easy in the afternoon, Ollie was afloat in her bateau, casting into the Folly River. A quick flip, a splash, and she just saw the end of a spot-tail bass. She rebaited the hook, cast off, and waited.

In the blink of an eye, the line shook, and the fight began. That bass pulled, but Ollie pulled back, till finally she hauled it in. She took it home, cleaned it, fixed the fire in the hearth, fried the whole fish up just fine, and ate one side of it piping hot. When she had her fill, she suspended the remainder by the tail from a hook she had impaled in the wall beside the chimney. Hanging up there against the wall, the fish stared back at Ollie with only one eye. The large black spot on its tail stared back like an eye, too. Ollie decided to name her trophy "Ol' One-Eye."

The den of thieves—Barbarosa, Ferret Face, and Stump-Foot—having heard of Ollie's lone self and word of her concealed cache, aimed to make an assault. They would each be willing to give every eyetooth they had for her unaccounted wealth. They conspired to plunder as if they were the Union high command.

Not that this would do them much good. The Union high command had a low record of success in the Lowcountry. Back in June 1862, the Yankee army attacked Secessionville on James Island, next door to Folly, only they soon retreated, limping and licking their wounds. In April 1863, the U.S. Navy floated a fleet of ironclads up the channel to annihilate Fort Sumter, but they left dented, bruised, and beaten. Three months later, the army assault at Fort Wagner on Morris Island, the barrier island at the harbor's mouth next to Folly, became a Federal fiasco. As a result of all this frustration, that August the Yankees started shelling the city of Charleston. Terrorizing the civilian population and tearing up private property throughout the South would continue till the end of the war. Actually it would continue long after, if you consider the Reconstruction era.

Well sir, those three thieves assumed they could unearth Ollie's valuables and leave her none the wiser, or else leave her beneath the sand. Waiting for a moonless night, they collected croaker sacks, spades, lanterns, and liquor, then marched to the north side of Folly. They had done enough speculating about what they would find and how much it would be worth; they hoped the sacks weren't too few or too small. They got to joking about the good use they would put to the "Gilmore Rifles." That was the nickname cast upon the digging implements, in honor of Union general Quincy Gilmore, who was in command with more of an engineering army than a fighting one. During the digging of trenches on Morris Island, the Yankees turned their spades so much that today all that's left of the place is a glorified sandbar.

From the intelligence they had gathered and the faint light amongst the shadowy shrubbery, the intrepid trio could just make out Ollie's hut. They sweated heavily from the trek, the anticipation, the alcohol, and the August Lowcountry humidity. It ain't the heat that'll get you, it's the humidity; though sometimes what'll get you is stupidity.

Barbarosa broke the silence, giving the first order of business. "All right, lads. You, Charlie, go on up there, put an eye out, and see what she's up to. Be careful."

Stump-Foot Charlie hobble-hopped across the sandy landscape in the dark, trying to avoid tree roots and vines. Creeping up to the hut, he made his way around to the chimney till, lo and behold, he spotted a small hole in the wall. What luck! Instead of peering through a windowpane, he could spy on Ollie without being seen. Charlie hugged the wall and placed his face against the hole to see what he could see.

What he saw was Ol' Ollie, sitting in her rocking chair, darning a sock. She made no sudden movements and gave no indication that she was aware of a visitor; she just sat rocking and darning by candlelight. Suddenly she stopped the rocker, collapsed the darning into her lap, hunched up her shoulders, stretched out her arms, and yawned. That gold tooth in her wide mouth made a fine shine even by candlelight. Ollie looked over to the dried spot-tail bass hanging on the hook by the chimney, which just so happened to be near that eyehole where Stump-Foot stood watching her from the other side.

"So, here comes the first li'l visitor tonight," Ollie said. "Well, when two more of y'all come for company, I'll fetch my carvin' knife fo' a last li'l bit of work on ya before bedtime." She laughed.

Stump-Foot jumped like a spooked rabbit. His eyes went wide, ogling every inch of the hut. He stumbled back, staring at the wall and panting hard. Then he heard the rocking chair creaking again, but nothing else happened.

An owl hooted overhead, breaking whatever spell held Stump-Foot. He hopped, skipped, and jumped back to his comrades. Out of breath, all he could muster were a few words. "She . . . hag . . . knows . . . all . . . wall . . . knife . . . hag!"

"What did you see?" asked Ferret Face.

"She's surely a witch!" Stump-Foot cried. "She's a hag! She can see through the walls!"

"Oh, come on, now," said Barbarosa. "What did you see?"

"I been back of the chimney peekin' through a hole in the wall," said Stump-Foot, "only she seen me, through the wall! But that ain't all. It's what I *ain't* seen what convince me. She ain't got no blue on that house. Not on the shutters, doors, or anywhere!"

"What's that got to do with anything?" asked the sergeant, his good eye a-glaring.

"That be hag blue. It be the very color of Heaven's skies and Earth's water, so no hag can cross it. You trim your house in hag-blue paint to keep out the hags and haints, only she ain't got none on her house. She a hag, all right. She'll hex us or kill us!"

"What?!" exploded Barbarosa. "What are you goin' on about? Oh, hell, never mind. Private, you go. That's an order."

Private Ferret Face snuck up to the hut, tiptoed around to find the chimney, and stuck his eye to the hole to observe. He saw Ollie slow the rocker, drop the sock, stretch, and yawn, now for the second time. Her eyetooth gave off a golden glint in the candlelight. Ferret Face nearly whistled as he let out a slow breath. Thinking that twice the look is better than one, he shifted his weight to switch the view to his other eye. Ollie stared at the spot-tail bass hanging on the wall; inches away on the other side, Ferret Face eyed her through the peephole.

"Now, now, here's the second visitor come tonight," she said. "Lordy, when one more of y'all come to keep me company, I'll fetch my knife and do some carvin', yes, yes. You'll see." She laughed again.

Ferret Face started. What? he thought. She knows I'm here? She can see me? Through the wall? It's a spell! She *is* a witch! She's got the sight!

He fled from the hut, a picture of pure fright running through the brush back to the other two. He looked as pale as steam. He took three swigs from a bottle in his coat and stuttered a half-coherent report.

"She saw me, I swear, she saw me! I watched her watch me! Through the wall! And a knife, she mentioned a carvin' knife! She's a witch. She's a witch, all right. Charlie's right, I'm tellin' you!"

"You're mad, man!" said Barbarosa, disgusted. "You had too much to drink tonight! Honestly, I swear, youse two ain't worth a flea on a fish! I'll go see for myself."

Off went Sergeant Barbarosa, angry as a fire ant, striding across the sand, with his long red beard waving like a banner and his one good eye scanning every dark object in his sight. He trailed around to the chimney, located the peephole, and pressed his one good eye to the aperture. Witch? Hag? Ha! So far he had survived the war, and he would get to the bottom of this business, too.

There sat Ol' Ollie, rocking back and forth like a metronome, darning a sock. She rocked and stitched, rocked and stitched, rocked and stitched, till Barbarosa had to rub his eye from the monotony of her movements. When he looked again, Ollie stopped the rocker, dropped the sock, and yawned the third and last yawn of the night. Her gold tooth caught the light—and caught the eye of Barbarosa. He grinned from ear to ear as he sighed in satisfaction.

That's when Ollie said, "Well, now, let's see. I mark the third of you three visitors come to keep me company tonight. So, now it's time; it's time."

Barbarosa froze when he heard that. How did she know I was there? he wondered. Did she really have the sight? Could she be an actual witch, a hag?

Ollie rose from the rocker, put the darning in a basket on a table, picked up a long, heavy knife, and turned to look square at that wall-mounted spot-tail bass. Eyeballing the wall where Barbarosa hid, waving that knife, Ol' Ollie smiled wide, saying, "All right, now, time for a little bedtime snack. Hang on there, Ol' One-Eye, till I cut me out a hunk of meat." She laughed.

Barbarosa couldn't believe his ears. He couldn't believe his eye. With her gold eyetooth glinting in her grinning mouth and that mean-looking carving knife gripped in her hand, Ollie was marching across the room to gut him, right through the wall!

When Ollie was almost on him, Barbarosa turned and ran blindly through the dark woods, no words for a scream. He ran past his buddies, who looked after him with blank stares. Spooked by his fear, they ran after him into the darkness. Not a one of them knew where they headed, only that it was away, far away, as quickly as possible, from Ollie in her hut.

Back at the hut, Ollie enjoyed her usual nighttime chaw of spot-tail bass as she reclined under the covers of her bed. With the last satisfying swallow, she sighed and smiled. Then she leaned over to the little side table by her bed and blew out the candle. Soon enough, she was sawing logs.

Days later, a squad of Yankee sawyers hauling logs by wagon across a sandy causeway in the spongy marsh caught sight of something unordinary. As they sat atop the wooden load, they spotted three distinct dark spots on a distant sand dune, only steps away from a darker morass of pluff mud. Beyond that, the Folly River swept out to the Atlantic Ocean. The three dark spots turned out to be dark-blue, government-issue, enlisted men's caps, two with insignia for the 100th New York, the other for the Second South Carolina. The sand looked disturbed right down to the pluff mud, where something recently had passed through. It didn't seem as though whatever it had been got very far. Pluff mud's only about one grade thicker than quicksand.

The midafternoon sun, humidity, pluff mud richly redolent of salty sea and swamp, and an electric buzz in the air all combined to give an eerie feeling to that sight at that site. The squad of Yankee tree-cutters didn't stay there long. They collected the caps and reported the materials found.

As for those three notorious boys in blue—Barbarosa, Ferret Face, and Stump-Foot—they were never really missed. The official accounts and muster sheets for the 100th New York don't list as "missing in action" either a Sergeant Barbarosa or a Private Ferret Face. The Second South Carolina don't include no Corporal Stump-Foot in its list of missing either.

Nobody knows for certain whatever happened to Ol' Ollie. Some folks claim she still haunts the island, but whatever for ain't known neither. I guess it'll be a secret still. One thing for certain is all them Yankee soldiers were gone with the winds of time. Yet now you know how at least three of them got served some Southern hospitality by Ol' One-Eye Ollie of Folly.

> *"In sum,"* I told Jim, *"from the fortunes of war,*
> *those three thieves got shortchanged!"*

CHAPTER 4

The Silverware Civil War

For once, the Lowcountry Liar got the chance to listen to me tell a tale from my family's archives. No doubt, he'll be telling it somewhere, sometime. You can too; help yourself.

Ninety years before I was born, Union general William Tecumseh Sherman had his bluecoats burn Columbia, the capital of South Carolina, my home state. That's a fact. Not being there at the time, I cannot recall details, but many memoirs and history books provide eyewitness accounts. The records make fascinating reading. There is one story of that time known only to my family that no historian has ever documented nor described. It was an odd occurrence, a small skirmish between the scourge of the South, General Sherman, and my great-great-uncle James McCréight of Winnsboro, South Carolina.[1] It was about spoons.

They met in early 1865. Sherman's invading, ravaging Yankee army had already torched Atlanta, giving a different meaning to the expression *Hot'lanta*, and marched across Georgia to the seacoast to have Christmas in Savannah. By mid-February, Union forces occupied Columbia. For several days, the Yankees pillaged the property and terrorized the citizens at the center of Secession. Then the army moved north towards Winnsboro, a quiet village but the hub of commerce for Fairfield County, as well as a key railway link for the state.[2]

On February 20, 1865, the first Yankee soldiers entered Winnsboro. These bummers, or land pirates, did not march in as a unit but came as marauding bands of greedy individuals intent on plunder. They began to pillage and terrorize Winnsboro, taking whatever they pleased. The hapless citizens were defenseless; all able-bodied sons and fathers were off fighting for the Confederacy. That left only the elders and youngsters, women, and the maimed to take on the daily chores necessary to maintain their homes. When the rapacious, demonic bummers arrived, bent upon destruction without discussion, the good folks of Winnsboro could do little to combat the calamity.

The bummers were zealous in their official capacity as foragers, taking as the Federal tithe enough food to feed the whole town for a year. Whatever livestock was deemed unfit for feeding the Feds was left for the folk of Fairfield County. After the bummers ransacked the town, some gathered at Winnsboro's market square.

Three historic sites bordered the square: the courthouse designed by America's first architect, Robert Mills;[3] the imposing Sion Presbyterian Church; and the town-hall market with its big French clock ticking away in a tower about as tall as the said church's steeple. Before these venerable buildings, the bummers built a solid mound of meat. It was an ugly pyramid. It was perfectly good food, too—whole hams and sides of bacon. The bummers set it ablaze, a nasty barbecue. Now no one could eat any of it, yet nobody could stop the fire. By the light of the flames, the bummers staged mock snowball fights with flour stolen from a local mill, covering the square with a fine white dust, a faux snowfall.

Well, war or no war, such a willful waste of food was considered obscene by the hardworking, God-fearing inhabitants of Winnsboro. The thievery was injury enough, but such wanton destruction was beyond insulting. All over town, Sherman's bummers carried off valuables and heirlooms, and whatever they couldn't take they broke up or burned down. Thus was the epithet "damn Yankee" cruelly earned.

This overly aggressive action was uncalled for, but with the local men away, there was no forceful authority on hand to halt the harassment. Some men who *could* fight were lying low in hideouts, worthless cowards who were dodging Confederate conscription crews. There was hardly an adult male voice with a Southern accent left in Winnsboro.

It seemed that the only safe way to control these wastrel soldiers was to plead directly with the Union commander. Although with little trust in true bluecoat justice, the folks of Winnsboro still held out hope for the return of their stolen property, once Sherman showed up. The meantime truly was a mean time—a terrible ordeal. The bummers had set some homes afire, and a burning warehouse full of cotton bales flared angry red and orange flames. The billowing smoke could be seen for miles.

The smoke got Sherman's attention. Soon, the first companies of his far-flung command came marching up the south side of town. These were disciplined troops, marching in step, glad to be part of such an army. Even though they were also the enemy, some folks in Winnsboro felt relieved to see them, believing that relative order would be restored and possessions returned.

A volunteer committee of three Winnsboro representatives hastily assembled to meet with the Yankee commander and help oversee operations. One of the volunteers certainly knew about operations, a physician, Dr. Horlbeck, who weighed over three hundred pounds. Another of the three gentlemen was an Episcopalian minister, a Reverend Lord—honestly, that was his name. The third member of the committee was my great-great-uncle James, a successful merchant and artisan, one of the town's most illustrious citizens, and a lifelong resident of Winnsboro.

Standing under the town-hall clock, in the main market square, the ad-hoc committee awaited Sherman himself as the blue troops passed by. At last, the general's staff appeared, with lots of gold on their shoulders, and then, there he was, Maj. Gen. William Tecumseh Sherman in all his dusty glory. The reverend, the doctor, and my great-great-uncle James approached the commanding officer in measured steps. The good reverend led the way, as he liked to get to the point. His parishioners said that his sermons were shorter than any other local Sunday speakers. That's the story that was passed around, anyway, but who knows? We were Presbyterians.

"General Sherman!" called out Reverend Lord. "General Sherman! We three citizens of Winnsboro have been appointed to represent the populace. As such, we respectfully request that you enforce control of your troops! Put a stop to this unholy marauding! It is the lawful thing to do! It is the moral thing to do!"

General Sherman was taken aback. He hadn't expected to meet much resistance, let alone holy resistance, and certainly not at such close quarters. His staff was equally amazed. One officer began to draw out his saber as he urged his horse towards the trio.

That's when two things happened, almost simultaneously. My great-great-uncle James stepped up in front of Reverend Lord, having to dance a brave little two-step around the doctor before the horseman's approach. At the same time, General Sherman reached out, grabbed, and jerked the bridle of the advancing officer's horse. The belligerent bluecoat lurched forward in his saddle, mashing his face in his horse's mane, and his saber dropped back into its scabbard.

"Captain!" said Sherman. "This appears to be a parlay, not an engagement. Did you not notice this man's collar? Let's hear what the committee has to say, shall we?"

The brash captain blinked and nodded, looking sheepish in his saddle. Without a word, he suddenly pulled his mount's reins sharply to the right and trotted off to survey the train tracks behind the market. Sherman and his staff watched him ride away.

"Ah, cavalrymen are always so impetuous," sighed the general.

"Born to the saddle but not very subtle," muttered my great-great-uncle James. He looked up to see General Sherman staring at him.

"And now, gentlemen," said Sherman, "if you would be so good as to introduce yourselves. It seems apparent that you already know who I am."

"Yes, we do, General," James replied. "Allow me. This is Reverend Lord, of the local Episcopal, see. And this is Dr. Horlbeck, an eminent M.D. of the town. I am merely Mr. James McCréight, a local businessman and *cabinetmaker*. I am known for my woodworks and a carpentry shop."

"I see," said Sherman. "Well, gentlemen, you all have your credentials. What is it you wish to discuss with me?"

"General, there are no troops here except yours," said Dr. Horlbeck. "And as I have myself witnessed, your troopers have acted abominably! Such loutish behavior! The brutal destruction! The outright theft of property!"

Reverend Lord spoke up. "Your troops, General, are running amok, despoiling everything! They frighten our families and expose them to terrible calamity!"

"Ah, 'tis the spoils of war, gentlemen," explained the general.

"Well, your boys have just about spoiled everything we've worked for," James answered with a little touché in his tone.

General Sherman was about to say something more, but instead shut up, and looked again at my great-great-uncle James. Sherman leaned back in his saddle, scanning the scene around him. The pile of burnt food smoldered and stank, oozing greasy streaks into the streets. The heat from the burning cotton warehouse lent a balmy air of summer to the wintry February surroundings. Orders were shouted from afar, soldiers rushed along the streets, and shocked citizens were fleeing from every quarter. The reign of terror continued.

"General, your bummers—ah, your men—have locked me out of my shop," James said. "They took my keys. They have probably taken all of my tools, too."

Sherman, his eyes black as onyx, stared at James.

Stepping up his complaint, James said, "The bummers have also stolen all of our family's silverware from the house!"

At this accusation, the general replied, "Perhaps you have mislaid your plate?" Several horsemen chuckled and grinned at Sherman's inference that we had buried our family treasures. Great-Great-Uncle James must have smiled.

"I assure you, sir, that my foragers are under orders," Sherman claimed. "Even the worst of these 'bummers,' as you call them, wouldn't take *all* of your silverware. You must have other eating utensils, besides—surely some everyday flatware."

"No sir," James replied. "My family and many another fine family here in Winnsboro have had to involuntarily donate from our kitchens every last knife, fork, and spoon, silver or not, to your Union army! Seems y'all are tired of finger-lickin' your food."

General Sherman was again about to say something but stopped himself; perhaps he was distracted. He frowned deeply and appeared to bite his lip. Perhaps he was sincerely worried about the wholesale thievery employed by his official foraging parties. All rumors aside, even the official reports made note that the practice was out of hand. It was plain to see all the way from the Savannah River to Winnsboro.

Before Sherman spoke again, my great-great-uncle James put his own plan into action, an offensive defense. He would use it to put the Yankee's army at ease.

"Of course now, General," James volunteered, "I could turn a lathe to make some wooden spoons and forks, but I would have to have access to my shop and tools. As it is, I'm locked out. By your men. Under your orders. I'm barred from my livelihood."

Sherman listened with tight lips and tight eyes.

"If not wood," James said, "I suppose we'll have to get by with our bite-size spoons."

"Your what?" Sherman asked. "What kind of spoons?"

"Our family's homemade, bite-size spoons," James explained. "You might call it an old family recipe. It's a remedy we've used plenty before. May be our only solution." Or salvation, James no doubt thought.

"What do these spoons look like?" Sherman asked. "What are they made of?"

"Well, General, I could show you," James offered, "give you a demonstration. In fact, our whole family could show you, General. How about you and your staff here come on over for supper tomorrow, around three o'clock? We'll need a little time to rustle up enough food for y'all." James smiled, shrugged, and spread out his arms.

General Sherman glanced at the greasy, smoking pyre in the square. He raised an eyebrow, then raised an arm and summoned a colonel to confer with for a moment before sending him off on some order. Sherman leaned over in his saddle, the leather creaking, and spoke to the committee.

"Gentlemen," he said, "after considering your situation and my timetable, a short respite may be in order." Then General Sherman addressed my great-great-uncle. "Mr. McCréight, my staff and I would be honored to dine as your guests. I have just ordered my commissary quartermaster to requisition ample enough foodstuffs to provide a stew for the meal. I'm afraid, though, that we will not be able to furnish you with any of the necessary eating utensils." Sherman paused and forced a grin. "But as you say, sir, you do have spoons." Sherman's staff nodded and grinned.

"Yes sir," James said, "we've got spoons enough to spare for every bite we take."

Sherman was startled when he heard this assurance. His grin disappeared, and his eyes glared wide. He looked at his staff. They were surprised and curious as well. One or two of them laughed aloud.

"All right then, sir," said Sherman. "My mess cooks will arrive tomorrow before noon at your residence to set up preparations. My staff and I shall join you and your family promptly at three o'clock for supper."

With that, General Sherman spoke sharply to his staff, ordering all larcenous activities to cease and an inventory of whatever materials had already been confiscated or stockpiled. He directed some officers to command bucket brigades to fight the fires and rescue any threatened buildings. He recalled the contentious cavalry captain and gave him the thankless task of overseeing the cleanup of the square.

The restoration activity by the erstwhile hooligans brought some relief to the townsfolk. Maybe after all this mess there was some justice attainable; after all, it was high time to build trust between assumed enemies. That night the citizens of Winnsboro slept with a bit more security than they should have expected from the Yankees.

Meanwhile, the McCréight family was bustling about, having to first find, then set up, a long line of tables in the spacious backyard and collect any available crockery, all while gingerly smuggling to the house highly prized ingredients from secret caches. When our family built the house, we had constructed a big brick oven adjacent to the house, on the north side ironically, where we baked more than enough bread for our family, and so we customarily baked for neighboring families too. We literally ran our bread business "on the side." Now finding the family in dire straits, we needed to use all of our resources, and so by the end of the day, we were prepared for the morrow.

Not long before dawn of February 22, the very birthday of

America's first president, my great-great-uncle James arose from bed, dressed, and went outside to the big brick bread oven and rekindled the fire. He left the warming oven long enough to fetch his elder daughters from their beds. James had been a widower since his dear Rachel left him over a dozen years earlier, but with six daughters among his offspring, the household held up well. The girls, already expert bakers, organized the production of bread dough in the crowded kitchen. There was plenty of dough, too.

We ground flour at our own mill out on Jackson Creek, but we kept most of it in secret snug spots just outside of town that we had also used during the American Revolution. General Cornwallis and his redcoats had occupied Winnsboro during the winter of 1780-81. Now the invaders wore blue coats. Neither time did it matter the color of the uniforms. What mattered was the uniform shade of inhumanity displayed by those who wore them.

Anyway, the daily bread had to be made. James returned outside to regulate the heating of the oven. By the time it was toasty and ready for toasting, the girls had the first batch of bread dough ready to go.

The entire family baked bread all morning long. The finished loaves, emitting an aroma of hearth and home, were stored in the parlor on the south side of the house. That may sound odd, but no one was sitting around in the parlor, and we needed some secret place to keep the bread warm. Our family had built the house with two chimneys, one at each end.[4] The north-side chimney with the kitchen hearth was used year round for general cooking, and the south-side chimney with a hearth on the ground a floor below was used during the winter to heat the whole house. We had built our homes before in both Ireland and Scotland in the same manner, so we continued the tradition in America.

By noon, when some of Sherman's staff rode up, the parlor was knee-high in loaves of freshly baked bread. The whole house smelled of warm wheat. My great-great-uncle James gathered the family together in the kitchen to share a prayer. Then he gave everyone a nod, a wink, and a thumbs up before he hailed the soldiers.

The major in charge was all business as he ordered the mess cooks to arrange large pots and set up cook fires at the far end of the backyard, well away from the house. He ordered another squad of soldiers to erect a tent over the line of tables, which ran east to west, from the back of the house almost to the cook fires. The opposing seating arrangements were oriented along a north-south alignment, which was only fitting.

An hour after arriving, the Yankees had the tent pegged, the cook fires crackling, and an aroma of beef and barley emanating from the steaming pots. We secretly finished baking the last batch of bread, quietly knocked down the fire, cleaned up the kitchen, quickly washed up, put on Sunday clothes, and set our side of the tables. As hosts, we took the north-side seating, so with the Yankees facing us, all parties could face their respective homelands. We were just trying to be polite. Lastly we brought to the table a covered hand wagon packed with loaves of new bread.

At three o'clock, three dozen officers, from the general himself down to a couple of captains, rode down our street, clip-clopping and clanking in a splendid military display. The soldiers on duty at the house saluted; the cooking staff was told to carry on. We all nodded to our guests and spoke pleasantries, but no one shook hands. My great-great-uncle James made excuses for Reverend Lord and Dr. Horlbeck. They both had to attend to their respective flocks in town, as there were calamities aplenty. No specifics were mentioned, but some of those officers would not look at us eye to eye. When we invited our guests to their seats, General Sherman placed himself at the center of the tables, and his staff spread out to his left and right. My great-great-uncle James sat opposite the general; the rest of the family, with a few friends and neighbors, sat opposite the officers.

The Yankees eyed our place settings, that is, our long line of various and sundry plates and drinking cups, sans cutlery. Then, as if on silent command, Sherman and his staff noisily pulled out their mess kits of pewter plates, tin cups, and full sets of fancy personalized dining utensils. Right there before us, at supper in our own backyard, our uniformed Northern guests displayed their regalia of forks and knives and spoons across the tables. Some of the smug brass hats smirked; some of them, like Sherman, seemed to be downright curious to see our family's bite-size spoons. We showed no response to the present company's swaggering array. Then the general made a personal proposition to my great-great-uncle James.

"Mr. McCréight," said Sherman. "May I address this issue of your allegedly misappropriated silverware?"

"Yes, General," said James, "by all means, do."

"Well, it may be that we have discovered your missing property among some contraband items that we came across in our scouting and foraging. However, all such materials are under guard at a separate location, pending proper identification. You understand." He grinned as if he was trying to kill us with his condescending kindness.

"Well, of course, General," James answered, "but that's business for later. Right now, supper's ready, and I believe that is the only business any of us should take seriously for the time being. Too bad y'all didn't bring a piece or two of the silverware for us to see, but I understand, we all do, that y'all been busy."

"Well, sir," Sherman said, slightly stung, "as you yourself claimed, Mr. McCréight, your family has enough spoons to spare for every bite they take."

"Each and every bite, General, that's a fact," James assured him with a smile. "We have spoons enough to spare for every bite we take! A spoonful, a bite!"

"Yes, well, in that case," Sherman addressed James in a stiff official tone, "my staff and I would like to see proof. So, sir, a proposal. Are you a betting man?"

"Look around you, General. You see my assets, most of them anyway. So what's not to gamble?"

"Answer a question with a question," Sherman said, grinning again. "You are a clever man. No doubt your people came from Ireland, like mine."

"That's true enough," James replied. "We came over from Donegal, up from Clare.[5] I am in truth but a humble carpenter, sir. Yet, you deem me a clever man, I know how things stand."

"Yes, well, we propose to dispute your claim," said the General, "and we will bet you that you cannot make good on it."

"And the wager is—our silverware?"

"And the wager is—" Sherman stroked his whiskered chin "—your silverware," he agreed. Some of his officers chuckled; some nodded soberly.

James said in measured tones, "That's a risky ransom. But you know, General, with so many witnesses to this wager, I'm reassured that you will honor the bet."

Great-Great-Uncle James stuck out his right hand to the general. For a moment, everyone looked at his arm stretched across the table like a bridge. Then Sherman reached out his right hand and shook on the bet. The so-called social ice may not have been broken, but it was showing a crack, starting to thaw.

"And now, General," James announced, "let us say grace and break bread together!"

Everyone bowed heads, some of our family and friends giggled as they all held hands, and my great-great-uncle James spoke over the meal at hand. His words were brief; a breeze replied with the aromas of hot stew and freshly baked bread. With an earnest "amen" like a collective sigh on our side, we all relaxed our grips, though were anxious to eat.

The cooks came around with serving pots full of steaming beef stew. They ladled out full measures to Yankee officer and Southern host alike. At the same time, the McCréight girls uncovered the hand wagon to bring out trays and baskets brimming with fresh home-baked bread. They distributed loaves to every diner on our side of the tables and put out several more for our guests. The bluecoats noisily helped themselves, quickly getting busy banging their cutlery, chewing, and talking loudly. After the bread was given out, my great-great-uncle James pulled out his pocketknife, which made General Sherman stop chewing, his fork in the air.

"Oh, not to worry, General. It's just my whittlin' knife. Told you I was a carpenter." James winked. "And it's my game piece for a friendly round of mumbly peg."

Sherman grinned widely and nodded, then renewed his chewing. As James sliced into a loaf of bread, a wisp of wheaty steam escaped. He cut a thick slab from the loaf. Then he tore off a quarter of the warm slab of bread and looked across at General Sherman, who stared back.

Cupping the bread, James dipped and scooped up a spoonful of stew. Then he bit off the mouthful of bread and stew and sat back, enjoying the repast. He daintily touched his fingers to his lips. General Sherman sat stone faced.

All along our tableside, we were tearing off hot slabs of bread and scooping out bite-size morsels of the Union stew. As we ate quietly, the officers began noticing our eating utensils. Some of the soldiers sat with their mouths agape—and some hadn't finished chewing—others had their forks full of food hanging in midair. They all were amazed, maybe shocked. Our "proof" was in the pudding, so to speak.

We went on eating, commenting on the hearty quality of the stew. Since the source of the meat was local, we thought it best to politely compliment the cooks. They all shook their heads at first, then nodded and smiled back. James scooped up a bite of stew and looked across at General Sherman.

"Can I slice you some bread, General?" James invited. "We have plenty. We been bakin' all mornin'. Yes sir. Lot of loaves. We had to bake a lot of loaves today so we—"

"—*Could have spoons enough for every bite you take*," General Sherman finished for him. He shook his head, grinning from ear to ear, and put down his fork as if in surrender. He bowed his head and chuckled, actually chuckled with mirth. He looked up and down the tables, then rose from his seat. His staff began rustling to stand, but he ordered them at ease. Gen. William Tecumseh Sherman addressed us all.

"Ladies and gentlemen, please, if I may have your attention. As it is evident before us all, the staff of life serves each of us in various ways. It appears here that truly one man's staff is another man's dining tool. I salute you, sir, in your extraordinary choice of utensils. You no doubt designed this, ah, dinner plan, and we have been outflanked." General Sherman raised his tin cup in a toast. His staff followed suit.

We graciously accepted the recognition by raising our motley collection of cups and drinking saucers. For a suspended moment, nothing was said. But as soon as General Sherman sat back down, everyone broke out laughing. We all laughed like we hadn't laughed in nearly four years. There were tears, but these were tears of relief for a change, rather than tears of grief. I cannot deny that General Sherman wiped at his eyes, too.

Well, we ate a homemade bite-size spoon of bread with every bite of stew and even had seconds to finish that special supper. After the feast, the family still had plenty of bread, more than enough for every bite. When the Yankees left our home later that day, they were still smiling about it, even though they had lost the bet. My great great-uncle James had been true to his word about homemade bite-size spoons for every bite.

General Sherman invited my great-great-uncle James to come to the courthouse later that evening, to inspect the silverware stored there. James found only a pair of our silver spoons from a wedding-gift set. That's all the silverware we ever recovered from the Federal army's bummer raids. The rest most likely went to feeding any number of unknowing Yankees—perhaps even to this day.

That is one of my family stories, and it is a part of history, which until now most folks did not know. In February of 1865, we McCréights found out right at our own home in Winnsboro that the spoils of war do not by course lead to just desserts. Nonetheless, we came away from our supper engagement with Sherman with a sweet taste in our mouths, satisfied to have shared a right hearty laugh during the worst of times.

"I like your spoon-bread story," Jim said.
"Reminds me how the South shall rise again!"

Note

This is an all-American folktale, based on an obscure trickster tale from Mexico that spread throughout the Southwest. I blended the tale with accounts of my family's hometown experiences of February 1865 with Sherman's troops during "the late great unpleasantness." We call it our "skirmish" with Sherman.

That is when Union general William Tecumseh Sherman, occupying Savannah, Georgia during the Christmas celebrations, threatened Charleston. He wanted to catch the Confederacy in

South Carolina off guard from the coast to the piedmont, so he spread his army across the state in three columns. Everyone expected him to avenge the Union by invading the Holy City as the British had done and ravage the center of Secession. The general's objective was to shorten the war by shortening the maneuverable space for the shortening Confederate forces in Carolina. And he did.

Marching northwards from New Year's Day through Valentine's Day, tying up the various local Confederate forces while destroying or confiscating every valuable possession in sight, his troops stopped in Columbia, the capital, long enough to loot and torch the city. Apparently that was the goal all along, not Charleston. Sherman knew that Charleston already lay in ruins from the colossal fire of December 11-13, 1861, as well as from the continual Union bombardment that lasted from August 1863 through February 1865.

Continuing northwards through founding father George Washington's birthday of February 22, Sherman encountered my ancestor James and the committee at Winnsboro. My family helped stop the destruction of the town and lessen its suffering by ripping the general a new "rear ventilation duct," right in front of his men and the townspeople. Humbled, perhaps, or maybe just tired from traveling, Sherman ordered a cessation of destruction and disenfranchisement of property in Winnsboro. Then he and his troops moved on to Camden and Cheraw, South Carolina.

Ironically enough, McCréights have been mayors of these two towns as well as Winnsboro. Perhaps, in the mists of time back in ancient Ireland, we McCréights had committed some unmentionable but memorable transgression against the clan Sherman, and the general was chasing down my family, not the Confederate army!

Family history accounts that the Yankee bummers learned of our silverware hideaway when they overheard the location revealed by one of James' nieces (who married into the family). We have never seen our silverware again. They are heirlooms gone with the wind.

CHAPTER 5

To the Victor Go the Spoils

The Lowcountry Liar reconstructed this ghost story from the era of Reconstruction, wherein some acts are more grave than brave.

Back in the bad days following the uncivil war of Northern Aggression, countless covetous scoundrels, from carpetbaggers to congressmen to the boys in blue, were uniformly hell bent on keeping the South on its knees. During the era of Reconstruction—that is, the error of Wreck-construction—a peculiar happening happened in Charleston concerning the fate of a Federal soldier stationed there at the time. He was alike to many of them unkind, uncouth characters who tried like the Devil to use any means most unnecessary against the common good. The particulars of the happening have been recounted ever since then to become a Lowcountry legend. The following account contains elements as best as can be attested for true, by yours truly. I'll tell you as I heard it, just as if we are there.

Three Northern cohorts, Ed "Fingers" Finnegan, Walter "Dipper" Brown, and Tommy "Snooks" Fletcher, are standing each other rounds at O'Ryan's Star Tavern down in the Charleston market. The year is 1866, late in the month of October. In fact, it's the day before Halloween. New denizens like these three stout warriors from the North have invaded Charleston to reconstruct Southern society and corral unrepentant rebels.

"Ha, ha, ha, me boys, here's to our new digs!" declares Fingers. "Here's to the tarnished jewel of the South!"

"To the Holy City, our new home!" chimes in Dipper.

"You mean the Holey City," corrects Snooks, "after Sherman shelled it!"

"*Och,* he never did, you know," says Dipper. "That were Quincy Gilmore."

"Sure, another brave Irishman!" boasts Fingers.

"No matter," says Snooks. "The mere mention of the name Sherman is enough to make the walls crumble like ancient Jericho."

"To Jericho!" toasts Fingers.

They clank mugs together and drink, reveling in such repartee. All three are sergeants in the Federal occupation army of the republic. They are currently stationed south of the Mason-Dixon Line, not in their hometown of Philadelphia, for Pennsylvania no longer needs defending. They spend the days in Charleston shouting orders at lazy privates, cursing slow Negroes, and verbally abusing anyone without gold sewn on their shoulders. These three sons of the city of "brotherly love" sneer in contempt at any white Southerner regardless of social rank, with a spit in the street. Native Charlestonians, black and white alike, generally regard Yankee soldiers as being in step with the despised scalawags and carpetbaggers. The bad business practiced by the finagling financiers despoils the community, and bluecoats are seen as soiled uniforms wherever they go. Like the ubiquitous cockroach, the Federals have invaded practically every walk of life in Charleston, and the people see where they stand in the new social order of postwar South Carolina. The current state of affairs has all the apparent simplicity of thumbscrews, with the determining factor being whether or not your thumbs are clamped in the torturous device. These three stalwart sergeants avidly do their duty by turning the screws on Southern citizens.

"Another round?" suggests Dipper.

"Why not?" Fingers asks, with a detached air.

"Another round!" demands Snooks of the publican.

The publican, O'Ryan, an Irishman from county Clare, fills new mugs and brings the brew to the table. He winks at the sergeants and taunts, "These are the only rounds you boys are shootin' these days, eh?" They laugh at his good humor, loving the laugh and a boast to boot.

"Sure, now, Ryan," says Snooks. "You set 'em up, and we'll shoot 'em down!"

More laughter follows from the trio. O'Ryan—a veteran of the Mexican War, with nurtured Southern sympathies—turns aside to hide the smirk of disgust he bears these overbearing Yankees. Thinks he to himself: Wouldn't I like to wipe the pleasure off your gabbing gobs. Wouldn't I like to wipe up the floor with your like. Instead, he returns to the bar and pours himself a whiskey, the firewater of life from the motherland. Raising the glass, he toasts the bluecoats. *"Sláinte!"* he cries, and they return his salute.

To himself, Ryan is thinking: We may be brothers from the same old sod, but that's an island unto itself. Here in this new land, under this so-called Union, we're strangers. You blue bellies are unwanted occupiers, foreign invaders. Don't expect to understand. Don't expect to be understood.

O'Ryan pours himself another whiskey, drinks it down, then carries the bottle and three glasses over to the table of noncoms. They are somewhat surprised at his largesse, but they grin at one another as he pours each soldier a golden shot of the precious liquid. They grab the filled glasses, a-waiting a toast from the host.

"Me *boyos!*" says O'Ryan. "To the memory of the valiant fellows of our former homeland. Here's to the good Lord Edward Fitzgerald!"[1]

"Oh, aye," agrees Snooks. "To the United Irishmen!"[2]

They all gulp down the flame-flavored drinks. The soldiers, already well fueled, smile broadly, feeling the burn. O'Ryan refills the glasses.

"Here's to Wolfe Tone!" cries O'Ryan.[3]

"To those lost at Vinegar Hill!" echoes Fingers.

They throw back the whiskey. It races through the blood. The soldiers share a collective sigh, shaking their heads in sad remembrance. O'Ryan pours again.

"To the martyr, Robert Emmet!" O'Ryan nearly shouts.[4]

"Cut down in the flower of his youth," laments Dipper.

They drink, starting to feel the edge of numbness. The embrace of whiskey and Old World history leaves them stoic. Melancholy begins to seep into their sensibilities. Before long, they'll be singing maudlin songs of separation, loss, and despair, as the Irish are so well versed in. O'Ryan fills the glasses once more.

"And now, me boyos," says he, "here's to an Irishman like us. Though his roots were in Ulster, he was a son of America. He too is gone. He's buried right here in Charleston—in fact, right up the street. Here's to John Caldwell Calhoun!"

The three sergeants start to drink but catch themselves, spilling some whiskey.

"What?" asks Fingers.

"Who?" says Snooks.

Dipper is speechless, with a confused look on his face.

O'Ryan throws back his drink, lets out a satisfied gasp, and holds the whiskey bottle up like a beacon. "Now, lads," says he, "let bygones be bygones. *Is maith sin.* Y'all won the war. Can you not toast a fellow Irishman?"

"Calhoun?" queries Fingers. "John C. Calhoun? 'The Great Nullifier' himself?"[5]

"The very same," says O'Ryan. "And why not? He's as good and dead as any soul at Sharpsburg."

"You mean, Antietam," Fingers tries to correct him.[6]

"Dead is dead," replies O'Ryan, "no matter the name of your last restin' place."

Snooks starts to stand up, saying, "I think we've heard enough of *youse.*"

"Steady, now, *bucko,*" cautions O'Ryan. "Y'all may be off duty, but you're still in uniform. And every sergeant has a captain."

Snooks sits and looks at his companions, who shake their heads.

"Here, lads, to show I hold y'all no ill will, take the bottle," offers O'Ryan, "but be off with yourselves. Drink it elsewhere." He stakes the bottle in the middle of the table and folds his arms, awaiting a response.

"Sure, why not?" asks Dipper. "Haven't we got roll call early enough?"

"Yeah, sure," says Fingers. He swallows his last glass of whiskey. Then he sneers. "Antietam."

The other two spill the lively liquid down their throats. Fingers grabs the bottle and they all stand up. Pulling on their long blue overcoats, the three Yankee sergeants teeter through the door of the Star Tavern. They weave through the market and wobble down deserted Queen Street. They upend the whiskey bottle among them by turns and, before they know it, wind up before St. Philip's Episcopal Church.

"Hey, fellows," says Fingers, "ain't this the church where Calhoun's buried?"

"Could be," says Dipper, passing the bottle to Fingers. "Yeah, I think so."

"Where are we?" asks Snooks, disoriented.

"Yes sir, I believe this is the church," announces Fingers, still fuming. He spits out, "Episcopalian! Ulsterman!" He takes a swallow from the bottle, sizing up the edifice as if it would speak, equal to his own defiance.

"See there, the bell tower?" Dipper points upwards. "The Rebs used it like a lighthouse to signal blockade runners. We used it as a target. Yeah, this is the church."

Snooks looks up, trying to focus on the steeple, but he stumbles backwards. He is stupefied with drink, literally blind drunk. The other two grab his elbows to steady him and he nearly slips out of his army-issue overcoat.

Dipper says with mock authority, "Sergeant Fletcher! Sergeant, you are extremely off duty!"

"At ease, soldier," says Fingers.

Between them they settle Snooks on the sidewalk, propped up against one of the church columns. They drape his uniform overcoat across him like a blanket. Snooks passes out, asleep in fumes of alcohol.

"Och, another casualty of the *poteen*," observes Dipper.

"Aye, and here's to ya," salutes Fingers. He takes a long swallow of the redeye, nearly emptying the bottle. He passes it to Dipper, who frowns but upends the bottle to finish it off.

"There now, Dipper, on to new business," says Fingers. "What say you and me reconnoiter the perimeter? Keep an eye out for unfriendly pickets."

"What's that?" asks Dipper, confused.

Fingers winks at him. "Let's you and me, Dipper, go dig up ol' John C. Calhoun!"

"What?" asks Dipper, his eyes wide.

"Sure, wouldn't the Great Nullifier himself like to see what's become of his special city by the sea?" proposes Fingers. "And wouldn't he like a full, free breath of the night air? Ain't it refreshin'?"

"Aye, 'tis fresh enough," Dipper agrees, "but do you not think it desecration to dig up the dead?"

"It's John C. Calhoun, man! What honor do we owe the likes of him?" Fingers asks with mischief in his eyes.

"I know who you mean," says Dipper, "and I know what you mean. Still, man, 'tis the dead. Let him rest. He's been dead for what? Fifteen years? I say *requiescat in pace.*"

"Come on, now, boyo," soothes Fingers. "We'll not steal his bones. I only want to talk to him. Tell him a thing or two."

"You're mad, you are," says Dipper. "Let me remind you, there is martial law here. We could be shot by our own boys, or maybe lynched by these Southerners."

"Or we could have a tale to tell beyond belief!" Fingers exclaims. "What, are you scared, Dipper?"

"You know that's not true!" claims Dipper defensively. "C'mon, let bygones be bygones. Like O'Ryan said, *is maith sin.* It's all good. Let it be, man."

"To hell with that Mick!" says Fingers angrily. "He's all pie in the sky. Like they say down here, that dog don't hunt. Get me?"

"You're wrong, Fingers,," warns Dipper.

They eyeball each other—comrades, brothers in arms—sizing up the situation. They lean in to each other, closing the gap. Their breath escapes in ghostly puffs of steam into the chilly night air.

"The whole damned war was wrong, me bucko," argues Fingers, "but that didn't stop anyone from fighting, now did it? So, are you with me?"

"I am, so I am," says Dipper. "God help me, I'm with you, Fingers."

"Good, then, let's go," Fingers commands.

"What about Snooks?" asks Dipper.

"Leave him," says Fingers. "Ain't he as good as dead himself?"

"Right enough, he is that," Dipper agrees.

The two sergeants amble along the sidewalk and cast-iron fence in front of St. Philip's Church. Surrounding the holy edifice on three sides, and across the street in a separate lot, lie past parishioners in their eternal plots—among them John C. Calhoun. A soft breeze rustles the stark limbs of the few trees left standing in the dual cemetery.

Finding the iron gate padlocked, the sergeants inspect the high iron pickets of the fence between them and the church-side graves. Without hesitation, they hoist themselves over the metal spikes and drop with soft thuds into the graveyard. They scan the street for activity, but no alarm is raised; only the naked limbs of a crepe myrtle tree rattle like bones. A light wind crosses through the cemetery, lifting and settling the branches of a large magnolia tree with a sigh. From the iron bars of the fence, a rosebush languidly waves a few tendrils in the air.

"Would you look at this, now?" asks Dipper, amazed. "A rosebush here with the dead, and it blooming." He pulls a bough near him, sniffing the red flowers. "Glory be, there's life with the dead."

"Glory damn be," growls Fingers. "Enough of the hor-tee-culture. Let's find Calhoun's grave! I want my say."

"That won't be so easy, you know," Dipper warns. "I heard these Rebs moved him to an unmarked grave somewhere over here."

"Where was he?" asks Fingers.

"Across the street," Dipper says. "The Rebs moved him over here somewhere, for fear of the likes of us, don't you know?"

"Well, at least we're on the right side," says Fingers, and adds, "again."

Dipper smiles and says, "Sure, 'tis the luck of the Irish!"

They chuckle at the joke. Despite the sacred site of their search, the whiskey still holds reign over their senses. In a moment, though, the spell breaks. They try to focus, peering at the tombstones.

"You check up that side. I'll check this side," Fingers orders.

They part and begin a systematic survey of the stone markers. Dipper discovers the resting places of a pair of Revolutionary War heroes: Edward Rutledge and Charles Pinckney. He reads the historic details chiseled on the headstones, which bring a somewhat sobering light to the nefarious action now under way. As statesmen, Rutledge signed the Declaration of Independence and Pinckney signed the Constitution. In reflex, Dipper crosses himself and backs away. He looks across the graveyard, searching for Fingers, but cannot find him. He hears a shout, then spots a shadowy human shape waving to him from under a massive oak tree near the center of the lot.

"Dipper! Dipper!" calls Fingers. "Over here, man! I think I found it!"

Dipper runs over to Fingers, following the footpaths rather than passing over the plots. In deep shadow under the oak, Fingers has fallen to his knees atop a dark mound. There is no marker, but the smell of turned earth hangs in the air. It smells like a fresh-dug gravesite.

"Are you sure? Calhoun?" Dipper asks. "There's no markings."

"'Course not," says Fingers. "Why would there be? These Rebs want to keep it a secret after all, don't they?"

"Yeah, that's right enough," Dipper reasons, "but still, I don't know about this. It's getting late, and it's getting cold. We got roll call, and Snooks is passed out in the street."

"Well, *Mother,* if it's all too much for you," sneers Fingers, "then go on home. If you dare not do it, fine. I surely do dare. Beat retreat to the barracks, bucko. I'll do the bloody work. Go on—leave me!"

By the timbre of Fingers' voice and the enraged look on his face, Dipper is convinced to leave his friend to his fiendish work. The shadows and soundless aura of the graveyard surround the senses, too much to withstand, so Dipper begins to edge away. He ain't too intent to make this place his last stand. A crow caws suddenly, unseen from one of the trees.

"That tips the scales," affirms Dipper. "I'm off!"

"Never would I see the day when a thief like you lost his nerve!" Fingers spits out. "To hell with you, then!"

"To hell with you!" Dipper yells back, running amongst the graves. He clambers over the iron fence. There lies Snooks, as still as a sentry, but drunk beyond use. "Maybe O'Ryan will lend me a hand," says Dipper aloud. He heads back to the Star Tavern to request assistance.

Alone in the graveyard, under the solemn oak, Fingers searches for a shovel, any kind of digging implement, but finds none. Frustration mounting, he kicks the mound of dirt before him and curses the spot. He pulls a knife from his boot, plops down on the middle of the mound, and begins digging.

"Damn you, Calhoun," says Fingers. "And damn this place. Damn this night. Damn this knife for a damn shovel!"

Fingers digs for several minutes, but the whiskey and the work wear him down. Stabbing into the dirt, he only loosens more soil that he has to bail out with his bare hands. Wind slips through the trees like a soft parade, limbs waving in silent salute.

"If I can get me hands on you, Calhoun, I'll wring your damn dead neck!" promises Fingers. "I'll take this knife and take off your head, so I will!"

Sweat rolls down his face; his uniform is damp. He raises the knife, stabbing again and again, but no box is found. "Aaaarrrrgh!" cries Fingers, anguished, furious, and frustrated. "Come up, you bastard! Come on up here, John C. Calhoun, and fight me like a man! I'm calling you from your own grave! Answer me!"

Fingers stops digging to catch his breath. Nothing stirs around him. Only his heavy breathing appears like an apparition as the air escapes him in regular streams of steam.

"All right, then," Fingers says finally, "you'll not come up. No gentleman's duel. Fine, then. You can take me blade to your black heart!"

Knuckles white, Fingers grips the knife and thrusts it to the hilt into the hill of dirt. He heaves a heavy sigh, as if his work is done. Then he spits on the ground before him.

"Take that!" he shouts. "Take my curse! And take my knife, you cur!"

He sways some and shakes his head to clear it. When he starts to get up, something halts his progress. Something is pulling at his overcoat. bending him in a hunchback position. He is unsure what's happening. The crow caws again, above in the oak.

Fingers freezes in place, his eyes wide. The wind is still. The night is silent.

"What in the name of Heaven?" he questions. "Sure, now, what's got me coat?"

Fingers falls on one knee. He cannot stand. An unease begins to grip him.

The night wind blows across the lot, waving tree limbs as if taunting him. Bare branches clack together like bones. Something—a twig—whips by, stinging his cheek.

"God help me," says Fingers. "God, no!"

He tries to stand again, but something holds his overcoat, pulling him down again. Now fear, a palpable feeling, races up his spine. Panic seeps into his psyche.

"No, God! I didn't really mean it! I swear!" Fingers avers. "Calhoun be damned, but don't you damn me!"

Again he tries to rise, and again he fails. Something—someone?—has an iron hold of his overcoat and won't let go. The sweat of fright mixes with his sweat of toil. He pulls off his cap and beats the mound of earth.

"Let me go! Let me go!" he shouts, louder and louder. "Damn you to hell! Let me go!" He flings the cap cross the yard and runs his hands through his hair, pulling at it. "Dammit, I survived the bloody war! You can't take me like this!"

All his wailing and flailing are useless. He's trapped on the little hill of real estate. In anguish he cries and tries once more to stand but cannot. Fear, panic, and dread well up in him. He grabs at his chest, excruciating pain a-pounding there. He can't stand it. He can't stand up to flee. A last gasp of living breath escapes him.

Fingers collapses across the grave. There is no movement, not sound.

Entering the Star Tavern, Dipper seeks out O'Ryan, who is surprised to see him return alone. He offers to pour a beer, but Dipper waves his hands no. He motions for a quiet word with the publican.

"What's eatin' you, man?" asks O'Ryan.

"I'm needing your help," begs Dipper. "Can you come lend me a hand? Snooks is passed out drunk, up by the church of St. Philip, and Fingers, well—"

"What is that *eejit* up to?" O'Ryan asks, his eyebrows raised.

"Well, he, that is, we, started to—well, I left, only he stayed," explains Dipper. "I have no stomach for the like. Call me superstitious, or no, but—"

"But what, man?" O'Ryan is getting testy.

"We climbed into the graveyard," Dipper admits. "Like it was a bet, a dare. We were trying to find the grave of John C. Calhoun."

"The *Divil*, you say!" exclaims O'Ryan. "What are ya goin' on about, now? Did y'all think you'd see his ghost?"

"I don't know what we thought," admits Dipper. "I'm sure I don't know what to think. Or what Fingers was, I mean is, on about. He was more than drunk, I tell you."

"Good Lord, man," says O'Ryan, exasperated. "So now you want me to help you get this *amadán* buddy of yours off the holy ground?"

"Couldn't you now, O'Ryan?" Dipper pleads. "He's just up the street."

"Well, in the first place, I don't close for another hour," O'Ryan states. "Then I'm havin' to clean up. And there's the inventory and the stockin' up for tomorrow. You boys in blue have a powerful thirst on you these days."

"You mean, you won't help me," Dipper realizes.

"What would you have me do?" queries O'Ryan. "Isn't it enough that your boyo crossed a sacred line? And couldn't I be shot or arrested, tryin' to fix your mess?"

"All right, then," Dipper says, resigned. "So you will not help us. I swear, I can't convince anyone of anything tonight. Oh, to hell with the lot!"

"Here, now, no hard feelings," says O'Ryan. "I'm tied down here, so I am. Why not let your pals sleep it off till the morning?"

"They'll be late for the roll call," says Dipper.

"So?" asks O'Ryan. "So, they'll be late. What's the harm?"

"Dammit!" curses Dipper, slamming his hand on the bar. He looks steady at O'Ryan and exhales deeply. Then he turns away and walks out of the Star Tavern.

Dipper returns to a snoring Snooks, now supine on the sidewalk. Peering through the iron bars of the fence into the darkness of the graveyard, Dipper cannot discern any human form. He dares not scale the fence again. He hasn't the will nor the energy. He pulls up Snooks and drags him back to barracks.

Come the morning, at roll call, Dipper and Snooks call present, but Fingers cannot be accounted for. Snooks has a massive pain from his hangover. After a dose of the hair of the dog, the two sergeants make a beeline back to St. Philip's Church.

As they come upon the churchyard, they see civilians crowding the street, watching something through the fence. The sergeants step down the footpaths with eager pace and anxious face. Surrounding a large oak tree in the center stand church elders, municipal officials, and military personnel. The sergeants smartly salute superiors, then worm through the crowd till they reach the mound of dirt.

Splayed out atop the grave lies Sgt. Edward Finnegan, aka "Fingers" to his mates. His hair has turned white as new snow and his face almost as pale. His expression looks like a mask frozen in terror: mouth agape and eyes almost bulging from the sockets. It is a wholly horrible sight, as abject an object as any casualty witnessed on the battlefield.

Dipper and Snooks gasp. They stare in alarm at the stark cause of death. There, for all to see, buried to the hilt in the dirt, stands Fingers' knife. Pinned beneath it is part of his great blue overcoat.

"*Jaysus,* Mary, and Joseph," says Dipper. "He stuck himself to Calhoun's grave! He scared himself to death!"

I didn't dare ask Jim if that was the meaning of the old saying, "the South shall rise again!"

Note

Here's an old chestnut of a ghost story. There are variants with men, women, or teenagers using knives, forks, walking canes, etc. The reference to John C. Calhoun is connected to a Charleston legend, and he rests, we guess, there still to this day.

The cemetery of St. Philip's Episcopal Church is the resting place for many important Americans, from the Colonial and independence eras through the antebellum and Secession times into today. Tour guides will show and tell you about local ghosts there, but rarely is this tale heard in the light of day or night. I tell it whenever I can—and dare.

PART II: THE GOOGLY

CHAPTER 6

The Edisto Crypt

The Lowcountry Liar narrated this unnatural occurrence during a day trip we took out to Edisto Island. The place he mentions in this story still exists intact, should you wish to visit there yourself. It would be best not to go alone.

Some folks say this story is true. Some don't know. Most speculate.

It's generally accepted that the most common fear we humans share is death itself. Some say it's second only to the fear of public speaking. I don't know exactly where you'd rank a eulogy. It seems like that's the worst of both fears, but that's a debate for a later date. Somewhere along this dreadful line of thought lies the horrible fear of being buried alive. There ain't no doubt that's a hideous kind of hibernation.

As a case in point, a particular tragedy in the 1840s took place on Edisto Island, out by the Presbyterian church. You can't miss the church; you pass it coming and going on and off the island. The parishioners built the church back in the 1830s, a right impressive edifice of worship. But the church ain't the building in question; it's another structure on the church grounds you need to see. It's the marble mausoleum that's part of the bone yard, the stone house in the stone garden: the crypt.

The cemetery is laid out back of the church, where in particular stands the memorial tomb for members of the Legare family, erected right by the unmarked boundary with the surrounding woods. There's no fence around the resting place, just a close-cropped lawn that demarcates the dead residents from the live flora and fauna in the neighborhood. It's all as quiet as an unspoken agreement but as tangible a division as the Berlin Wall.

The French name *Legare* we pronounce "Legree," so that's what we'll use in this story.[1] We say a lot of French names in our own way. There's even a book to help you out. It's entitled *The Correct Mispronunciations of Some South Carolina Surnames*. I kid you not.

The Legrees were Huguenots, persecuted French Protestants who came over to the young Carolina colony to establish prosperous plantations while worshipping freely. The Legree family had money and prestige enough to have the special sepulcher of stone constructed. Compared to Egyptian pyramids, it's a miniature mausoleum, about the size of a tool shed. It resembles a sentry's guardhouse or tollbooth—plenty sizeable by the standards of Edisto folks and certainly fitting for the needs of the Legree family. Happily, only a few kin ever occupied that quiet stone house.

The Legrees had an island home, but they didn't live in it year round. Home sweet home was the big townhouse on the downtown Charleston peninsula, built with a couple of tons of bricks and heavy hardwoods and decked out with piazzas and tall impressive columns. There the Legrees dwelled most of the year till the high heat of summer surrounded everything with its inhumane humidity, creating an unbearable steam, a *miasma*, instead of breathable air. To add to the mix, every year from hazy June till the crisp cooling of October, some kind of epidemic disease, or a few, would take up residence amongst the residents of the hustling bustling port city. You could come down with yellow fever, typhus, cholera, diphtheria, a strain or two of hepatitis—heck, any sort of viral infection or bacterial outbreak could broom-sweep across Charleston. Any of these nasty elements could infect anybody, and any number of the folks infected would die.

Most of the Charleston elite lived south of Broad Street, an east-west avenue that cuts across the city. In that neighborhood, those folks have always been in *the haves* category, known for their wealthy ways—the blue-blooded, deep-pocket, high-cotton, bourbon aristocracy. The rest of us locals call them all "S.O.B.S.," for living high on the hog, *S*-outh *o*-f *B*-road *S*-treet. These same wealthy folks, who could more than enough afford any creature comfort, nevertheless had to suffer like anyone else in the good ol' summertime. All blood is red to the deadly mosquito.

During the hottest months, the better-off folks decided they would be even better off out of town. On various barrier islands off the Carolina coast, they built summer-home retreats that also stood as testimonials to the wealth of the owners. These houses weren't as openly ostentatious as the downtown domiciles, but they were elegant by any measure. Every one of them had a grand staircase stationed in front leading from the sandy ground up to the piazza on the first floor, ten to twelve feet high.

Edisto is a barrier island, which naturally could flood during storm surges. Typically the summer retreats were constructed with pillars, posts, pylons, and archways from the ground up to the first floor. The rest of the house stood on the raised floor, to keep the house cooler with the breeze blowing underneath. Now, that's adapting to the environment, especially the temperature; yet one of the reasons for having such a high house was the incessant plague of mosquitoes. It was believed that mosquitoes only flew close to the ground, so if you built your island summer home ten or twelve feet above the ground, you'd be safe from the itty-bitty biters for true.

Back then in the days before inoculations, nobody knew that such tiny critters carried big diseases. Nobody purposely sought out the deadly plagues of the pesky little humming bugs. Whenever people paused long enough to check the time, mosquitoes just naturally showed up uninvited to punch their clock. They gave us the malaria and yellow fever, taking out many citizens every deadly summer.[2] It used to be said we had only three annual seasons in the Lowcountry—a brief winter season, followed by a prolonged summer season with outbreaks of diseases, followed in the fall by the funeral season.

In 1849, Caroline DuBois of Atlanta, a Legree cousin, came to visit. Customarily she would be introduced as an Atlanta DuBois, signifying someone who hailed from a clan with lots of land and a solid reputation. An all-American Southern belle, Miss Caroline DuBois was a vivacious, affable, gracious, precious young lady of nineteen, with curly chestnut-colored hair and a rosy complexion to complement her robust character. Like visitors today, Caroline had a grand time in Charleston, whether seeing the Holy City's sights, or shopping, or dining. Her Lowcountry relatives wholly enjoyed her lovely, lively company.

Then the relentless summer heat settled in. The dire risk of catching some kind of mortal illness also settled in. Droves of folks of every denomination visited the many houses of worship located downtown in hopes of divine intervention as prevention. A visit to the doctor often meant it was probably too late for a visit to the doctor. What with the temperature rising, the general anxiety rising, and the ambulating, noisy crowds in the streets raising a constant cloud of dust, well, sir, it all added up to make living wholly uneasy.

The Legree family, including cousin Caroline, packed up, closed the townhouse, and moved out to Edisto, retreating for the summer. They enjoyed more greenery, fewer people, soothing sea breezes—all in all a markedly healthy change from the miasma of the city. The bonus of panoramic sunsets awash in magical rainbow colors inspired awe in every observer.

From the last half of July into August, the rains came. Every late afternoon, sudden thunderstorms let loose showers that soaked the spongy soil and filled the wetlands, raising the water level all around and afterwards leaving pools and puddles everywhere. When the rains stopped, the island seethed with a humid steam of air, an effluvial essence not quite as permanent as in the city, where it was mixed with constant human traffic. Despite the circumstances, and utterly unmindful of urban angst, the Legree family inhaled the idyllic island existence, enjoying the lazy life on Edisto. They ignored a particularly insidious aspect, that persistent pest, *genus aëdes*: the *mosquito*.

Anyplace where there is such heat and humidity and breezeless air, you will be sure to hear a buzzing at your ears. The cooler nights don't deter the attacks; they only make it impossible to see the attackers. Hardly nothing bars skeeters from sleepers. Back in the 1840s out to Edisto Island, a traditional *rice bed* would be draped with lacy lightweight curtains—a flimsy defense, for true, easily, breezily bypassed by itty-bitty biting bugs.

It must have been the last week of August when it happened. Cousin Caroline suddenly seemed a bit listless, not her usual gregarious self. She wouldn't eat much of anything and vomited up whatever she swallowed. One fresh morning, she didn't get out of bed. She complained of leg cramps and sore arms, as if she had been laboring in the fields. She had a fever and got the chills. This continued on throughout September, though she seemed to revive intermittently, alternating from a running fever to feeling clammy with sweat, then cold to the touch. And all the while, she drank only by sips, never eating much and struggling to swallow at all.

It was nearly impossible to keep up Caroline's fluid intake with her sweating out her fevers, soaking the sheets. She was too nauseous to take solid food, and anyway, the summer heat and humidity ruled out nourishment such as chicken soup no warmer than the same soggy tepid temperature filling every room of the house. Caroline couldn't even keep down water; she would only retch up bitter bile, known as "the black vomit." She got to looking hollow cheeked from the lack of fortifying foods. She lost color to her cheeks too—got as pale as a sheet of paper—till finally her complexion took on a yellow pallor. She had it now for true, full blown, the yellow fever.

The rest of the family felt nearly as exhausted caring for cousin Caroline. Somehow, not one other family member got sick. Maybe they were inured to the bug bites, being from the Lowcountry. Sweet cousin Caroline of the north Georgia pinelands must have been nouvelle cuisine to the clan of Edisto mosquitoes.

The Legrees whispered about Caroline's state of ill health, comparing day to day and hour to hour. With dreary deep concern, they worried over her as they waited for her to get well. Someone commented how the lace netting that hung roundabout her rice bed resembled a shroud. It seemed like a harbinger.

Finally, Cousin Caroline gave up the ghost. The Family Legree wept as much from grief as from relief. It was early morning on the seventh of October, 1849. That's just spookily ironic. As history would have it, that is the same day that the famous, or infamous, writer-poet-critic Edgar Allan Poe passed on. It might seem like a mysterious coincidence, and it does seem like more than random selection, but that's part of the whole mystery.

Isolated on Edisto Island, the nearest licensed doctors living at least fifty miles away in Charleston and busily fighting sicknesses in the city, the Family Legree was helpless to diagnose based only on laymen's medical knowledge. The servants had kept a respectful distance from Caroline, not wanting to mess with no mojo. Now she was cold to the touch, showing no perspiration or aspiration—bless her heart, she had to be dead. Her health failing all summer, Caroline's demise hadn't been unexpected. Still, death is always a surprise.

Down South in the summertime, you don't fool with the heat. Nowadays we have air conditioning to cool us off and refrigeration to keep meat fresh. Back then, they didn't even have iced drinks. So, a recently deceased body wasn't kept on display in the house for any lengthy viewing. The remains couldn't remain above ground in the broad daylight of a Lowcountry summer for long, not without malodorous consequences. And that ain't no way to be remembered.

At sundown that same day, after all the prayers and farewells were said, cousin Caroline lay encased in her casket. The Legree mausoleum lay open to receive another family member to forever lie at rest within its stone walls. They pushed closed the thick marble door and locked the grinding rock in place, and Cousin Caroline lay sealed up good. That's the last anyone saw of her, more or less....

Current events caught up with and overran the Family Legree, like most everyone else caught up in the chaos before, during, and after the War of Secession. The old family plot lay neglected while death was busy elsewhere. Time passed till twenty years later, in 1869, on the very same day it had so happened, the Legrees had need to revisit the hallowed family vault. They had brought home the reclaimed remains of a son who had fallen at Cold Harbor.

When they pulled open the heavy marble door, a collective gasp escaped the mourners. The coffin of cousin Caroline had been opened! Stretched full length on the floor, reaching for the door, lay her clothed skeleton. She had been buried alive!

Nobody moved for a full minute; they could only stare. Shock and horror, rolled over the crowd gathered at the tomb. Imagine poor Caroline, waking up from a deep sleep to find herself in total darkness, as though her eyes were still closed. If she wasn't claustrophobic before, surely that coffin made her so. Imagine Caroline fearfully, frantically, finally opening the lid and climbing out of the dead bed box. Imagine the terror she felt finding herself in a stone closet without a single shaft of light, without a draft of fresh air, without any hope of help.

Upon inspection, they found that all the tips of her finger bones were cracked and shortened to nubs. The inside of the marble door was scored with bloodstained scritch-scratch marks. Cooped-up cousin Caroline had clawed at the door, no doubt for hours, probably screaming for her dear life till she became hoarse—all to no avail. Nobody came. Nobody knew. What could they do?

Well, what else could the family do but place her back in her coffin? With prayers and blessings, and a dreary dose of mortal shame, the Family Legree mourned poor Caroline's passing anew. By nightfall, all the deceased were encased and in place, and the crypt was closed, more or less. . . .

The sexton arrived at the Legree island home early in the morning a week later, imploring the family to come out to the vault to see the door—or rather, not see it. Somehow, someone sometime in the night had destroyed the massive marble door, reducing it to a pile of rubble. It looked as if a sledgehammer or two had done the deed, but such a racket in the night would have surely brought people running to investigate. The sexton, a devoted tee-totaling Christian who lived on the church property, never heard any unnatural noises in the night. It was strange, too, that exactly one week had passed since finding Caroline.

Family members stared at the rubble, shaking their heads in awe of the almighty force necessary to obliterate solid granite rock. It took a while for the shock to wear off. They rationalized, as we humans are so apt to do.

The night before, an earthquake, just a slight shake, had been felt in the vicinity. It was a typical Lowcountry tremor, no big deal, but noticeable. You see, the Lowcountry has another added attraction, that being the major earthquake fault line running beneath the pluff mud of the Ashley River.[3] Well, just as well hidden must have been a fissure somewhere in that granite door. Everyone figured that during the nighttime shakes, the split in the door expanded, and presto, the stone door came crumbling down. It seemed plausible enough.

The Legree men set to work constructing a new door of thick heavy oak wood from a freshly felled tree. They also ordered a new stone door of blue granite to be cut from the quarry up in Fairfield County. There's a big natural quarry there, and blue granite is the official state stone. In fact, you might find a piece of South Carolina standing in any stone garden in the country, it's that well known and well used. Durable blue granite has passed the test of time, more or less. . . .

Another week passed until the sexton returned, rapping on the Legrees' front door, shattering the stillness of the early morning. It had happened again. The wood crypt door had dematerialized. This time, it had been torn free from the hinges and tossed like a Frisbee some forty feet into the woods. A blazed trail of broken branches exposed the rough-hewn path of destruction. Again, the sexton swore he had heard nothing odd, no bashing or crashing.

After inspection—and after speculating that something from beyond might be busy in the night—they all concluded that the accident had resulted from selecting a young oak tree to fashion the replacement door. They figured the wood was too green and had swollen up in the heat and humidity until it just popped out, ripped off the hinges, and went flying into the woods. The physics and the forensics seemed to satisfy the shared rationalization.

The Legrees rushed down to a local blacksmith and fetched him to fashion a door of iron bars, like on a jail cell. He even drilled holes in the lintel for the fitting of a locking mechanism to drive the bars up and down into the doorsills. He constructed the door right by the crypt, using that oak door for firewood. Nobody talked much; they just watched the flames dancing as the smithy worked.

When they installed the iron door and locked it into place, they all said some more prayers for peace on the matter. The Presbyterian minister was there to say a blessing for the family, for poor cousin Caroline, and for the new iron door. Now for the most part relieved, everyone then went about their business, more or less. . . .

The sexton had his brother staying with him now to have another witness at the site should anything out of the ordinary occur. They hadn't seen any curious visitors lurking on the grounds, but it didn't matter. Three weeks after the discovery of cousin Caroline's skeleton, the sexton and his brother found the iron door barely hanging from the hinges, all bent up and twisted like a pretzel. Summoned once more, the Legree family gathered at the gravesite, a somber semicircle of siblings surrounding the crypt entrance, staring at the mangled metal. Since the sad reburial of poor cousin Caroline, no door yet had withstood whatever power guarded the portal to the mortal chamber.

Could it be cousin Caroline?

It didn't seem rational. Some unseen, obscene power, able to crumble granite, toss timber, and wring metal, had taken up post as some kind of guardian spirit to the Legree family crypt. And if it weren't cousin Caroline, it could only be something worse!

As luck, or fate, would have it, that very same day the fat slab of blue granite arrived on a freight wagon from the Fairfield quarry. The rock had been precut to the doorway's dimensions. A stonemason had come along to finesse the fitting. After clearing away the wreck of wrought iron in the doorway, they set to work setting up the new stone door.

On the day before Halloween, of all days, the new blue granite door finally was emplaced. Everybody knew the date, the eve of Halloween, but nobody wanted to make an issue of it. The crypt now had a secure door, had been made whole again. That's all the Family Legree wanted to be concerned with. The work and the worry had worn out everybody; now the hope of grace through the Holy Ghost could take over, more or less. . . .

It turned out that the only thing taken over was the door, once more. The next morning, the sexton, making his usual rounds of the grounds, stopped dead in his tracks when he came to the tomb. There in the doorway lay the new stone door split in two pieces, stacked atop each other like a giant sandwich. The sexton ran straight away to the Legree home and had the family running back before breakfast.

It became another busy day for the family. By sunset on

Halloween night, when the haints bring out the dead, the family had dug graves for all their loved ones once housed in the Legree mausoleum. They respectfully removed the coffins, lowered them into the ground, and finally tamped down topsoil in mounds over each one. Every person present spoke a prayer in turn, then collectively they sang several hymns before heading home. Nobody wanted to stand watch in that graveyard on Halloween night.

None of the Legree family experienced any uncanny happenings after the burials. To this day, there still ain't never been another door of any kind on that little stone house.[4] Poor cousin Caroline must have found her rest at last. However, she made her point with them destroyed doors. It was as if she was shaking a bony finger at her kin and warning: *don't you ever shut the door on a departed soul lest you know beyond a shadow of a doubt that they are good and dead for true!* Amen.

We were standing in the graveyard when Jim told this ghostly story. As he finished, a car noisily pulled into the parking lot of the church. There were Pennsylvania plates on the car and Jim said with a wink, "Foreigner." The first thing the driver asked us as he jumped out his car was, "Hey, is this the church where the door won't close on the tomb?" Jim and I looked at each other; I believe it was the first time I ever saw Jim utterly speechless. After a moment, he regained his composure and said to me, "Well, if even a Yankee knows about this crypt, then you know it has to be an actual factual true story." Jim waved the man over and began telling the tale anew.

CHAPTER 7

Love Stinks

The Lowcountry Liar disclosed these details about the most sensational murder ever reported in the Holy City. He swore he gave me the facts, nothing less, and I shared some family particulars that proved pertinent, too. We wound up with a ghost story in a story in a story, and then some, getting to the heart of the matter.

A week after Veterans Day, the Lowcountry Liar (Jim Aisle) and I happen to be strolling along Broad Street. We step into Jake's Coffee Shop for refreshments. Out of the blue, Jim asks me, "You remember the other day talking about duels down South, the Code Duello?"

"Oh yes, *The Code of Honor.* I recall."[1]

"Truly the rage of its day. Rampant throughout the land," Jim declares. "That Code Duello, it outlined the proper etiquette on how to shoot someone, should you so desire, and they had plenty of deadly desire back in the day. That Code blood-bound a so-called gentleman to follow suit in a dispute—sometimes commit legalized murder."

"Sad but true," I say.

"You mentioned your family had some part in the last official duel fought in the Palmetto State?"

"That's right. The Cash-Shannon Duel. It was the fifth of July 1880, right after Independence Day. I guess they wanted to wait until after they had honored the holiday with its legal fireworks before they set off their own lethal fireworks."

"Might say. 'Course, in context, that's the days of the wild, wild West. The famous shootout at the O.K. Corral happened the following year, a few days before Halloween."

"There you go."

"Tell me again 'bout your family in that Cash-Shannon Duel. Neither is your name."

"Not exactly. My Scots-Irish ancestors settled up in Winnsboro. My last name is McCréight, and it's often mispronounced with a long *i*, like *McRight*. But we've always pronounced it, as in Gaelic, as *McRate*. Say it like it's the number eight. We spell it that way: *e-i-g-h-t.*"

"You know, in the Lowcountry, that number would be pronounced 'a-yet'—two syllables. Anyway, go on."

"Sure. A young Mr. Shannon had lost most of his family during the Revolutionary War. He was sort of adopted by my great-great-great-uncle William McCréight, who was the first mayor of Winnsboro and held that office for fifteen years. Shannon eventually made his fortune, not unlike my family, manufacturing houses, furniture, cotton gins. We were what they called 'cabinetmakers,' or general-purpose carpenters.

"Shannon moved, like some of my kin, some thirty miles east of Winnsboro, to Camden. There he raised a family. One of his sons he named to honor his benefactor: William McCréight Shannon."

"And he's the fella who fought the duel?" Jim asks.

"Yes. His opponent was one Ellerbe Boggan Crawford Cash. Of Lancaster."

"With four names, maybe he felt he had more on his shoulders."

"It was said he was a highly prideful man."

"Hubris?"

"Who knows? He was known to have a temper, was a bit of a hothead. Apparently created mountains out of mole hills most of the time."

"Ain't it always the way?"

"This time was no different. The fine point that inflamed Cash was a minor note scribbled in the margin of a legal transcript that Shannon didn't even write. An assistant attorney did."

"Shannon a lawyer?"

"Yep. That being so, he wasn't what I'd call lily-white innocent and pure of intent himself. He had made enemies over the years through business transactions and legal decisions. In some people's view, an officer of the court is a scalawag in a suit."

"Well, you know what they call a thousand lawyers at the bottom of the ocean?"

"I'll bite. What?"

"A good start."

"Ahhh, should've known. Anyway, the two opponents, Shannon and Cash, were following the gentlemen's guidelines fixed by *The Code of Honor* and agreed to meet in neutral territory. They chose a site outside Bishopville, now Lee County. That was fitting, I suppose, since they were both old Confederate colonels. They met by the DuBois Bridge, which is ironic, too, for my family. After the Revolution, some of us relocated to the western frontier of Pennsylvania and helped establish the town of DuBois. Weird, huh?"

"Seems a sight more than coincidental. Only I don't believe in coincidence."

"Well, as far as I know, the only connection is the same name at both places. We didn't build the bridge, though I guess we could have. We did help build the town up there in what they call "Penn's Woods." In fact, our house still stands there in DuBois. It's called the Wigwam—but that's another story. Funny that *DuBois* means *of the woods*. Another odd occurrence, maybe?"

Jim smiles and prods, "The upshot of the duel been that Cash killed Shannon?"

"Uh, yeah. Shannon got off his shot first, but he had intentionally hit the ground a few feet before Cash. Some sand sprayed up, stinging Cash in the arm and face. He thought he'd been hit, so he plugged Shannon in the heart. It was a tragic loss. All in all, Shannon was a well-respected gentleman, family man, businessman, victim. Cash, of somewhat similar means, became renowned as the villain in the affair. The notoriety of the Cash-Shannon Duel led to state legislation outlawing the practice, and it turned out to be the last official duel fought in South Carolina. That's how my family's involved."

"That law banning public feuding came to be largely because of Captain Dawson," Jim claims.

"He's the newspaperman you were telling me about, right?"

"Yep. Cofounder, joint owner, publisher, editor of the *News and*

Courier, the South's oldest newspaper. He also was a family man and twice-wounded Confederate veteran. But Dawson wasn't his real name."

"What was it?"

"Austin John Reeks. Some name, huh? He was kind of to the manor born in jolly ol' England. To a respectable English Catholic family, way on back.

"As a young man, Austin John Reeks was a fairly successful playwright, though the family disapproved somewhat of his dalliance with the theater world. A career in the theater wasn't considered wholly respectable. Still ain't for some.

"When our War Between the States broke out, young Austin John Reeks was eager to lend both hand and heart to the Confederacy. Told his family he'd be off to join the Southern Navy. Ma and Pa Reeks were against his rash desire. 'Go, be an actor, a playwright, a musician,' they urged. Better a life in theater with all its fantasy and temptation than fighting for and against foreigners in a civil war. Lesser of two evils.

"Young Mr. Reeks could not, would not, be dissuaded. He was adamant about his decision, ardent for the cause. His folks finally said, 'Fine, if you must, you must, but first change your name.' Family honor and all that. He did. Came up with Francis Warrington Dawson, honoring a couple of uncles and the good St. Francis of Assisi. Don't know if that was his first communion name, but it would be his Confederate alias ever after. He would prove as true to his name as he was true to his word; he would be wholly *frank*."

"Ok, ok," I sigh.

"So, Francis Warrington Dawson shipped out with the Confederate Navy, later joined the Army of Northern Virginia and served with the artillery, got promoted to captain. He was wounded twice, captured but exchanged, and saw action at Mechanicsville and Fredericksburg and Gettysburg. After the war, he ended up here working for the *Mercury* newspaper, till he eventually merged local publications into the *News and Courier*. And with as strong an opinion as he had for the Confederate cause, proud to be serving in the ranks, he likewise had a strong point of view in print, which he proved, having the power of his own press. That press was located *rye-cheer,* literally where we are, in Jake's."

"Right here? We're talking about the place in the place? I don't know if that's random selection or fate."

"Well, we're here, ain't we? Might as well tell the tale."

"Fair enough. Go on."

"Dawson became one of the original Dixie Democrats. Part of what detractors called the "Broad Street Ring," a group of Lowcountry aristocratic types harping on a return to antebellum days. They backed Gen. Wade Hampton for the governorship during the contentious 1876 election. They created political enemies too, 'specially with the upstate crowd, them straight-laced Baptists, as well as with local blacks and a powerful rival mayoral machine."

"And Dawson wasn't from here originally, so that probably added fuel to the fire."

"Yes *suh,* he been a 'com-ya.'"

"Oh yeah, I've heard of that in Charleston."

"We got two kinds of people in the Lowcountry. Either a 'com-ya' or a 'been-ya.'"

"Strangers and natives, right?"

"Pretty much. A com-ya is someone not from the Lowcountry who moves in, 'specially if they 'come here' from north of the Mason-Dixon Line."

"Yankees, you mean."

"Yes suh. 'Damn Yankees' if they stay. If you were not born and raised here, you 'from off,' as we say. Most particularly you from off the Charleston city peninsula. Anyone who has roots in the Lowcountry is a been-ya."

"Because they have 'been here,' right?"

"Correct again."

"My family came to Charleston from Northern Ireland before the Revolution and settled a while in Winnsboro. After the Revolution and the Civil War, parts of the family left for other parts of America. I grew up in a navy family, but we were stationed here more than once, and I have since returned to the Lowcountry."

"Makes you a com-ya who's been-ya but 'left-ya,' then 'com-back-ya.'"

"I don't think they have that listed as a category on the census form."

"Likely not."

"So, Dawson, or Reeks, was a certifiable com-ya, a foreigner in a foreign land."

"He was living down South, but he wasn't from down South. Kept to his English ways, like always taking a cold bath, even in the wintertime; not that it gets as cold as England down this way. All in all, Captain Dawson was a well-known, if not popular, fella. Had a friend-to-foe ratio of about fifty-fifty. He was a newspaperman after all, an editor, a vet too. A man experienced, opinionated.

"With all that, Captain Dawson was a uniquely complicated mix of a proper English gentleman and strict Catholic residing down South, and in Charleston at that. He was a principled, moral, and erudite man. Captain Dawson was a modern man of genteel character, a product of the Victorian Age with its prim ways of civil behavior.

"As an upright productive citizen, he hated the practice of dueling by alleged gentlemen. As a veteran of America's bloodiest war, he'd seen death and destruction a-plenty. So as a civic-minded businessman of the media hell bent on reform, he wrote many editorials against all gunplay, and otherwise actively campaigned to end the barbaric behavior. His work paid off, not that he was looking for a pat on the back. In 1883, a few years before his death, he traveled to Rome to be knighted by Pope Leo XIII (that's correct, lucky number thirteen!) for bringing peace among his fella men, helping to rid society of a specialized sin."

"And that all came to a head following the Cash-Shannon duel," I plug in.

"That it did. So you see, in a kind of roundabout way, your family, by adopting the young Shannon, later on was at least indirectly responsible for disturbing the peace, which led to a peaceful resolution. Only, not quite."

"What do you mean?"

"Well, suh, the irony is that Francis Warrington Dawson, for all his good intentions and fine, positive results in the matter of fighting duels, would himself later be killed by a man with a gun in a dispute about a woman."

"Chivalry isn't dead."

"Maybe not, but it surely killed the captain."

"How did it happen?"

"The Dawsons hired a nanny for their two children, a young Swiss miss name of Hélène Marie Burdayron. A beautiful gal, by all accounts. Kind of woman give a man whiplash when she pass him in the street. Hourglass figure, but she wouldn't give you the time of day. That made her all the more tantalizing to men of strong temptation and weak temperament. A Swiss miss dish.

"One particular fella with a fever for foolin' around was Captain Dawson's not-so-neighborly neighbor, Dr. Thomas Ballard McDow. I'll call him "TB," like he's a disease, because he proved to be as deadly as tuberculosis. And him a doctor, too. Ironic, for true.

"He had a wandering eye. Folks said he didn't have much affection for his plain Jane wife; married for money. Well, that's between them, I guess. His daddy had been a doctor too but practiced upstate in Lancaster. This clan of McDows of Lancaster produced a long line of lancet-wielding professionals."

"Gosh! Like Cash. He was from Lancaster!"

"Actual matter of fact. This one son, TB McDow, faithfully followed in his daddy's footsteps, till he tripped himself up. TB graduated with honors, was also the valedictorian of his class at what's now the Medical University of South Carolina. Got his start in Camden, same town where you had family, same as Colonel Shannon."

"That's eerie how all of this connects, interlaces, dovetails—"

"Like I said, seems a sight more than coincidental. Can't say I know what any of it means, but it is right interesting to speculate."

"I'll say."

"Well, suh, here's what happened as I know it to be pieced together. McDow had his office at street level below his home on Rutledge Avenue, at the southwest corner with Bull Street. Dawson lived on Bull Street round the corner from the doctor. They were neighbors abutting each other's properties at Rutledge and Bull. No bull.

"Dr. McDow used his piazza to view the Dawsons' house and backyard, where Hélène Marie often played with the children. Then, when Mrs. Dawson went to New York to visit her sister, and the captain was busy at the newspaper, and the kids were in school, Dr. McDow made his move, or moves. Visited the Dawson home repeatedly, unannounced, solely to see and flirt with the sweet young thang next door. She really was a honey—foreign, exotic, an alluring prize in his malicious eyes. TB begged her to run off with him, even kissed her a couple of times. She wasn't for none of it, though no doubt she liked the attention, even from a married man. Maybe especially so."

"Who knows what secrets lurk in the human heart?" I ponder.

"No telling. Word went round the rumor mill till it got back to Captain Dawson. He was furious, with both the rumor mongering and the purported acts. It all offended his sense of decorum. The chief of police heard next from the captain, so the chief had a patrolman posted on the corner right at Rutledge and Bull streets."

"Oh yeah, there's a pharmacy at that intersection corner."

"Back then, too, and a grocery store. The cop on the beat there kept an eye on things, sort of like watching a pot set to boiling. Both Dawson and McDow were known to have short fuses. The captain had shown his grit, and some of his blood, on the battlefield, and like I said, he had a deep sense of honor and duty.

"McDow had previously—guess what?—fought a duel! Maybe a few, over to Mississippi. Some folks thought he self-medicated, too. Shades of Edgar Allan Poe, you know? And as a physician, McDow had performed—when not even the word was said—*abortions*, mostly among the black population uptown. It was also rumored that McDow had falsified death notices for black folks, in order to cash in on kickbacks from paid-off insurance policies. The doctor was right popular with some of Charleston's black folks."

"Sounds naughty, nice, and notorious," I interject. "Not exactly a shining example of an ethical professional. Nor a pillar of high society."

"All of it come to a boil, spilling over on the twelfth of March 1889. Bound to happen. The date's unremarkable, not quite yet the

Ides of March and within a week of St. Patrick's Day. Come to a sad, unavoidable outcome, like if you let yourself get head-busting drunk. You assassinate yourself.

"Captain Dawson left his newspaper office sometime after three o'clock that spring afternoon, rode the blue-line trolley down Broad Street, up Rutledge Avenue, got off at the corner with Bull Street. Now, right then and there he should have done like a proper Englishman—gone on home, had a cup of tea. It'd soon be four o'clock, traditional English afternoon teatime. Cup of tea would've calmed his nerves, soothed his sensibilities, might have avoided the whole mess.

"But Captain Dawson could be bull headed. Don't know if living on Bull Street had an effect, as if he chose his home address by design. Or it him. Or not.

"Instead he butts his way into Dr. McDow's office, beneath the piazza of the doctor's house. Dawson's taller, bigger, got maybe fifty pounds on the doc, and he's agitated over honor. That is, the honor of a young woman, Miss Burdayron. Dawson considered her his employee as well as a guest in his home. Equally she was a guest in his adopted country. She had unwittingly attracted the unwanted attentions of an interloper. The captain felt duty bound to extend his aegis and nobly defend her reputation.

"Notice I said the word 'aegis,' a shield, to use one of the terms of the times. See, I can be a little erudite, too. Weather permitting." Jim winks.

"Well, 'erudite'—that's a word that's a mouthful," I say. "A well-polished, educated term. Very well learned of you."

"Well, suh, there's more to learn in this story. Both men were married, with families; both men were professionals of long standing. Surely, the forthright editor thought that the good doctor would see reason, his reason, but if not, a threat of force could be introduced. Surely then Dr. McDow would be reasonable."

"Seems that the anti-duelist had a fighting attitude, about civil behavior and honor."

"Or a dishonorable, uncivil action as reaction. No suh, a tiger don't change its stripes, and a rattlesnake always bites. Too bad for Captain Dawson, he bit off more than he could chew. McDow always maintained afterwards that Dawson came at him with a walking cane, beating him cross the shoulders, back, arms. Said that only then he opened a desk drawer, pulled out a pistol, and plugged Captain Dawson in the midsection.

"Later at trial, McDow testified that the pistol had been in his pocket all along. That was a practice in common use among that clan of Lancaster McDow doctors. They practiced the healing arts while packing heat.

"The forensic evidence was interesting, too. No physician examining the doctor for bruises could find a single mark on him. The line of fire was questionable as well, never really determined if the captain was facing or facing away from McDow."

"You mean the doctor might have shot him in the back?"

"Like I said, never really determined it to full satisfaction. But bad as all that, with the science and logic and physics, there's worse. The almost burial of the body."

"The what?"

"Yes suh. The doc shot Captain Dawson. Didn't kill him outright. Yet did he render first aid? Treat him to triage? Stabilize his condition, fix him up?

"No suh, not a bit, not a whit. The good doctor let the decorated Confederate battlefield veteran, Christian-knighted anti-dueling campaigner, newspaper editor, and family-man citizen bleed out and die. The good doctor just sat there listening to the wounded man's labored breathing, what he later described as a low, dull sound—sort of like a ticking watch wrapped mummylike in thick muslin. McDow watched as Dawson expired, waiting till Dawson's heart slowed to a stop.

"Guess the doc was in shock. Why not? It *was* shocking to be physically attacked in your own home in the middle of the afternoon, and by a respectable gentleman no less, who professed peace yet had a temper. McDow felt he had been defending himself and his homestead from an intimidating invader during an unwarranted attack.

"So, what to do? McDow now had a six-foot-four corpse to conceal. So in a closet under the staircase, he dug a shallow grave, using his bare hands to pull up the soil. Dragged Dawson's body over to the hole and tried stuffing him into the makeshift grave. However, Dawson's bulk wasn't cooperating. Floorboards didn't lie flat, let's say."

"That's a shade of Edgar Allan Poe," I say. "He wrote a famous story called 'The Tell-Tale Heart,' where a murdered corpse is buried beneath the floorboards by the killer. And although he thought he'd gotten away with it, the killer's conscience gets to him until he falls apart, reveals the body, and confesses everything to detectives."

"Apropos. Maybe McDow knew the story. Could have. This all happened forty years after Poe died, and it's nearly exactly what McDow did. Only now, after the body won't—don't—fit, McDow's fit to be tied. He figured the jig's up and turned himself in to the police.

"That flipped a switch. Almost instantly, a whirlwind of speculating gossip swirled round the Lowcountry, swooping through the air and picking up steam till sensational newspaper accounts of the strange duel soon swept the nation, too. The sensation followed through a major trial held downtown, with reporters covering the proceedings for the big-city press from Chicago, New York, and Philadelphia."

"The Windy City, the Big Apple, and the City of Brotherly Love."

"Aha. Surely a big wind was made of the love triangle that was all about the apple of one man's eye. No love was lost at the trial, though. The jury had five white and seven black men. Presiding over the arguments was a judge by the long-established Carolina name of Kershaw."

"Kershaw? Like in Kershaw County, where—"

"Camden's the county seat. I know. The same Camden, where McDow come from—"

"Where Shannon was from."

"The very same."

"A coincidence?" I ask. "A co-inky-dinky. Could call it a hinky co-inky-dinky."

"I kid you not. Leading the defense of the doctor was another judge, the notable Andrew Gordon McGrath. This judge had been governor of South Carolina during the uncivil war, and before that he closed the Federal office in Charleston when Lincoln was elected president in 1860. McGrath committed the first real overt act of secession."

"That's weird, coincidental, with my family again. McGrath is an Irish version of the Scottish MacRea, and my name, McCréight, is in there between them both.[2] They're all different spellings of the same relative clan name."

"Relative relatives, huh? See, you're connected to this story, but you ain't in it directly. Good thing too. The trial was dramatic, as all the reports say, with respected medical professionals contradicting the forensic findings, with the testimony of the witnesses, with the questioning of Miss Burdayron, with Dr. McDow's defense testimony. Lot of fireworks, couple of duds.

"Couple of good quotes from the trial, though, as I recall. McDow supposedly taunted the dying Dawson. Told him, 'You have tried to take my life, and now I have taken yours.'

"That's pretty much a confession. Yet McDow never did deny the act; he always claimed self-defense. A man defending his castle. Even if he's in the basement.

"The defense attorney, Judge McGrath, gave the other notable quote. The prosecution had been trying to portray the vivacious Miss Burdayron like she was the nursery-rhyme Mary, who had lost her innocent lamb to the big bad wolf doctor. However, Judge McGrath would have none of it, and even counter-played a pun that referred to McDow's poorer uptown clientele. Said McGrath, 'If her character is to be whitened, his is not to be blackened.'

"That could have been another switch flipped. The jury reasoned it over and came back with a not-guilty verdict. Despite the dead-actual crime, and the character assassinations, let alone the fuzzy forensics, the deed was ultimately seen as one of self-defense. First time in this state that a mixed-race jury had acquitted a white man of a capital crime."

"That's amazing," I comment. "What a news story!"

"Yeah, well, wait for it," Jim cautions. "There's a follow-up story to the verdict."

"What happened?"

"Well, suh, it's a local Lowcountry legend that Dr. McDow met his own, as they say, untimely death, by, as they also say, his own hand. Interesting obit for the paper. Most folks noticed the death of Dr. McDow because of the whole sordid account about the nanny and Captain Dawson. It was a definitive dark end to a stormy affair. Yet, it wasn't no dark and stormy night when it happened. McDow's comeuppance come up in late June, during a Lowcountry summer heat wave."

"Doesn't sound like it will have a happily ever after, after all," I mention.

"Ever and after for true, but happiness is way too subjective. No, it was about *fifteen* years later, just after the century turned twenty, well after the dust had settled over the grave of Captain Dawson. Despite it all, Dr. McDow still lived in Charleston, in that very same house at Rutledge and Bull.

"His wife and child had long left him, though it had been accepted that they were visiting kin up to North Carolina. His practice had fallen off, especially in recent years, even though he still was popular with some of the city's black folk. Probably the trial and general tribulations weighed on his conscious day, as well as on his conscience night. Besides, the years were catching up, too. TB was in his sixties. Had some signs of failing health, mostly heart trouble. Make your own judgment about his heart trouble.

"Couldn't heal himself. Could be that all them things conspired to make up his mind. And so as to augment his anguish, or maybe to give him a foretaste, that summer of 1904 was one of the hottest, most humid, air-oppressive summers ever in Charleston. I'm a been-ya, so I know that sometimes the elements here can jump right up and bite you. Put you out of your right mind till you're left wanting to maybe put yourself out of your own misery.

"Local word has it that Dr. McDow, now down on his luck and all, went down to his office below his home. There, he once more dug out a grave, right in the same spot where Captain Dawson had been laid to rest many years before. Dr. McDow lay down in the grave and, using the same gun that he'd shot Dawson with, placed the barrel to his temple and blew his brains out.

"He allegedly did that sometime around Carolina Day.[3] That would be June 28, a local holiday, but he wasn't found till after the Fourth of July, a national holiday. Raised a real stank. Kee-yarn, you know? That certain bad smell of long-dead killed carrion. Can smell it upwind, it's so nasty.

"Weirdly, a year later, Dawson's married daughter purchased her earlier home on Bull Street, around the corner, as an investment in the real-estate market. Not much income ever came back her way from it, though. She always felt the place had been tainted by the name Dawson. That was her maiden name, but again, remember, not really."

"Yeah—"

"Remember the real name of her father, the English Catholic who assumed a name to join the Confederate military? The same fellow killed and half-buried in the basement of Dr. McDow's house. Well, here's the sweet irony, because remember, McDow would die there too, but unknown till the gag-choke stench of his bloated corpse laying in Chawl-stin's hot humid summer air brought discovery. The sweet, sweet irony is the name of the physician's victim that's so delicious: Austin John *Reeks*."

"Oh, no," I realize.

"I kid you not. Can't make up such facts. It's all just bizarre. What's more, folks who have lived at the McDow house since then have reported that on heavily humid hot summer days, and nights, there's still a stank that emanates from that part of the basement. Even after bleaching and fumigation treatments."

"That is truly awesome," I say, amazed.

"Truly Charlestonian," says Jim.

> "On a slow news day," I replied, "anything can happen, including you making the news of the day."
> Jim answered, "If it bleeds, it leads, but if you don't have anything nice to say, best not say it."

CHAPTER 8

Mother's Milk

The Lowcountry Liar dug up this account of pioneering days in America. As he noted, living was so hard back then that some folks gave in and "gave up the ghost."

Nobody rightly knows the whole story. Like any history, some details can only be guessed at, facts formed out of fog. In this case, you might say "her story," since it tells of a mother's ever-lasting love. However, not everything lasts forever, and this all passed some time ago; nowadays there's no trace of the place where it happened.

You could look for it if you've a mind to. Some curious archaeologist might try to locate the site, reclaim artifacts, and write up a report. Well, suh, he'd first have to drain Lake Marion. That ain't likely to happen, now that the area in question is a manmade New Deal project that creates electricity for the state. Shoot, Belle Isle Plantation, the home of the Revolutionary War hero whose name graces the lake, Francis Marion, the ol' "Swamp Fox" himself, lies under those lake waters.

Who knows, maybe Marion heard the story, too. He was around at the time, back in 1765, a decade before the Revolution started. That was right after the French and Indian War, with King George III of England in sole control of the North American colonies. Good King George forbid any of his subjects from moving too far west, so instead, some of the hard-scrabble rabble of Ulster Scots trekked southwards to become hillbillies, good ol' boys, or Southern belles.

Back up in Pennsylvania, the German immigrants, mislabeled as Dutch, had gotten kind of obstinate, feeling pressed in by the Presbyterians, so they closed ranks with Anglicans and Quakers under King George. They all had low regard for the highlander Scots.

They didn't like having a "Mc" this or "Mac" that as neighbors and wouldn't sell them land. The only nearby sites available to the McMacs encroached on the native Indians, who got all NIMBY minded. The Not-In-My-Back-Yard attitude ain't nothing new in America.

The Scots-Irish, or Ulster Irish immigrants, most likely being Presbyterians who believed in predestination—that what be is meant to be—up and left the narrow-minded crowding-out attitude of the ensconced English and German settlers of Penn's Woods. The McMacs migrated to the promising land down South, especially to South Carolina with its tolerance of religion and plenty of wide-open spaces.[1]

They were a spirited and spiritual people, a spunky bunch. Such spark is a strong trait of the Celts, taking the hardships that come and never saying die. They had a strong belief connected to this tangible world, as well as to the unseen heartfelt world of life's essence. Back then, you would have to have more than a road map to reach South Carolina from Pennsylvania. You would have to have a gritty spirit to get you through rough pioneer trails.

Well, suh, that's some actual factual background history leading us to what else happened in the story. I admit, some of what follows is speculation, but most likely it's what occurred. Like I said at the beginning, nobody rightly knows the whole story.

A young husband and his very pregnant wife, a very new Scots-Irish family, traveled down the Shenandoah Valley of Virginia, making for Carolina. Somewhere south of Salisbury, North Carolina, the Cherokee took to ambushing parties passing through, and they must have waylaid this party, too. The husband died from his wounds, possibly near the Waxhaws, a rough settlement in Lancaster County, South Carolina, at the North Carolina border. Apparently the wife became a new mother following that traumatic event, maybe near Camden, South Carolina.

The area that today is under the waters of Lake Marion back then was full of frontier farmsteads. Somewhere in the vicinity, James and Sarah Moore had a place, with plenty of space for crops and livestock. They had no children as yet. They were busy enough keeping stock of the stock, tending crops, and fostering the faith in the community as active church members. Sarah often helped mothers cope with newborns, sharing the care of the other offspring. The Moores were nurturing souls.

The Moores also witnessed the parade of families passing on to hopefully better pastures. James and Sarah charitably helped out with food, a secure spot for a short rest, and a prayer for a future home. On occasion, James and other elders had to oversee the final ceremony for a hapless migrant who succumbed to sundry mishaps on the road.

A lifeless woman and her newborn daughter were found as if they were sleeping, lying in a wagon off the road. It must have been a fever they had that kept others away. The child couldn't be but a couple of weeks old. The mother, a young woman, looked tired from wear and tear, maybe worn out from countless tears shed over grueling hardships. She was worn out like the weathered wagon, the bruised box that held her, torn down to the few articles beside her. They were two more lost souls on the road from Pennsylvania. A ragged bloody shirt, probably her husband's, showed that he had been killed. Nobody knew their names, only that they had been part of the exodus, and this was as far as they could get. James and the other elders sadly laid mother and daughter to rest together in a simple pine box, placed at the far end of the church graveyard.

Now, things be in this world, and things be of it, and something strange, set between the "in" and the "of," came to be from that burial. Before sunup the day after the interment, an odd feeling, like a spider crawling across his shoulders, came over James as he worked in the barn milking cows. He hadn't heard nothing, only the cows making the usual milk-me moo songs.

James looked round to see a young woman standing by the barn door. She didn't say nothing, didn't move, just stood by the barn door, quiet as the fog hovering silently over everything in the early-morning hours. At first, she blended in with the fog, and James wasn't sure he saw her. Her dress and the shawl around her shoulders were as gray as Spanish moss. She wore a wide-brim, low-crown straw hat, commonly called a *Bergère hat,* popular with women of the yeoman class, the hardworking class. It appeared as moss gray as the rest of her ensemble. She wore big-buckle shoes, well worn and scuffed. Everything about her looked road weary.

"Good morning," James hailed her. "Can I help you?"

She didn't reply, just stood there in the grayness of the morning, still as a tree.

"Miss?" James addressed her. "Or ma'am, is it? I don't believe we've met."

The gray woman raised an arm, pointing at James. Slowly, nervously, he stood up, nearly knocking over the stool. He took a step towards her. She still pointed, but at the stool, then at the cow.

"What?" he asked her. "What do you want?"

She made no reply. She moved not a muscle. Like a tree limb, her arm pointed at the cow.

"The cow?" James asked. "You want the cow? No, the milk! You want milk?"

The gray woman nodded. James stared at her, unsure and uneasy. She turned her head slightly to look square at him.

"Yes," she said finally. "Milk."

James nodded back. "Sure, well, all right. I don't mind sharing a little milk. I'm sure the cows won't, neither, heh-heh."

His good humor made no impression on the gray woman. She didn't lower her arm till he sat back down and began milking again. Filling the pail, he asked her, "Ma'am, you got something to carry this in?"

She held out a copper canteen, wrapped in a wet gray cloth.[2] James took it, ladled milk to the brim, and plugged the cork into the neck. He nodded.

"That'll do you, ma'am," he said. "And don't you worry about a thing. I don't expect nothing in barter. It's just neighbors being friendly."

The gray woman took the canteen from James. She looked him square in the eye again and nodded. "Thank you," she said,

"You know, if you'll just hold on, I'll fetch my wife," James offered. He bypassed the woman and went into the house. In a minute he and Sarah stood at the front door, peering across the yard to the barn. The gray woman had vanished.

"Where'd she go?" James asked, astonished.

"Maybe she's just shy, James," Sarah told him. "Let it be. It's all right."

James scanned the yard and searched the barn but found no one else as the sun came up and burned away the fog. He shrugged it off and went about his business chore after chore, not thinking anymore of the gray woman.

But she showed up again the next morning. It was as gray with fog as the day before. Again, as James began milking the cows, he felt a presence but didn't hear anyone's approach. He looked up and around to see the gray woman once more at the barn door.

"Oh!" he started. "Well, morning, ma'am. I didn't know you were there. Didn't know you'd be back."

She made no answer. She stood tree quiet, gray as the fog.

"Well, then," said James, "do you need more milk?"

The gray woman again raised an arm to point at the cow. She nodded. "Yes," she said somberly.

James smiled. "I don't mind, ma'am," he told her. "I truly don't. We have plenty. Well, that's to say the cows have, but I'll fix you up."

Again, his little joke brought no reaction from the gray woman. James milked till the pail filled. He turned to the woman and saw she already held the canteen out to him. He ladled it full, corked it again, and handed it back to her.

"There you are, ma'am," he said. "Can I fetch you an egg or two? The hens might mind, but they always lay a gracious plenty. Wait you here; I'll fetch you some, fresh."

He crossed the yard to the hencoop. When he returned to the barn, the woman had disappeared again. There was no trace in the fog. He had no idea where she had gone.

That evening at supper, James told Sarah that if the woman came again, he would follow her. Not to demand anything from her for the milk—he was just curious about her.

"Well, you be careful, nonetheless," Sarah cautioned him. "She may be passing through and don't have a cow to milk of her own. Lord knows where her husband can be. These folks on the road may seem harmless enough, but you never know."

"It'll be all right, love," he assured her.

The next morning, the fog filled the farmstead as before. James sat milking but kept looking over his shoulder, expecting to see the gray woman any minute. Suddenly she appeared at the barn door. James jumped up.

"Well, good morning, neighbor!" James greeted the woman. "Thought you might come by again. I got a full pail already waiting for you."

The gray woman extended her arm. James took her canteen, filled it once more, corked it, and returned it to her. He smiled and shook his head.

"I declare, ma'am, you ain't much for conversing, but you do have a way without the words."

James chuckled, but the woman did not react. She just stood silent. Finally she nodded to James and turned to go.

He didn't try to stop her. This time he watched her cross the yard. She moved as though she was gliding over some smooth surface, like ice. Just before she melted into the fog, James shook with a shiver. He didn't know why, but it roused his spirit. Shaking his head as if throwing off a spell, he followed the gray woman.

She moved swiftly down the road and seemed to flow effortlessly through the woods. James followed at a distance, close enough to keep her in sight but not so close that she would notice him.

Finally, she stopped. James halted, too. The gray woman turned slowly and looked behind her. James darted out of sight behind a fat oak tree. When he dared peek out, the woman had gone.

The fog thinned some as daybreak neared. James cautiously stepped out from behind the tree and tracked where he thought the woman had walked on. He knew she had to be nearby, somewhere.

Now that he could see, he noticed he was near the church. He thought he saw a movement to the back, by the graveyard. He followed round to the spot.

There was only an unmarked grave, freshly dug. James thought it seemed familiar.

Then, he heard an odd sound. Strange, it seemed an almost human noise, like a . . . muffled cry?

James listened with all his being. The fog cleared, and the first ray of daylight shot across the sky. Yet, oddly, no birds sang out.

Then it began again, that odd muffled sound. The sound was at his feet. James looked down at the gravesite. The sound came from there, for true.

"My God," James said, worried.

Before he knew it, he began clawing at the grave, dirt flying everywhere. The muffled, grunting sound continued. Looking up and round, James spotted a shovel by another plot. Quickly he fetched it and began digging into the earth with all his might.

He found the coffin. He knocked it with the blade of the shovel, but only a hollow echo came back. He knocked it again. This time the cry of a baby replied. It was a baby, for true, but still muffled, like from inside that plain pine box.

James cleared the coffin and pried off the lid. What he saw there nearly made him faint. He felt—fear? Relief? Both? He couldn't tell.

There in the coffin lay the gray woman. She didn't move or open her eyes. There, clutched in her arms, lay a wiggling baby girl, only a couple of weeks old.

By the mother's side was the canteen, heavy, wet, and full to the brim with fresh milk.

"Well, I'll be," whispered James.

The baby squealed. She squirmed in the new day's blinding light. James reached down and gathered her up. She was warm. He grabbed the coffin lid, slid it back in place, and kicked some dirt to cover it.

James rushed back to Sarah. She couldn't believe what he held. The baby cried out, loudly. Sarah took her from James.

"She's hungry," Sarah declared. James ran to the barn to fetch more milk. Sarah sat feeding the baby girl.

Well, suh, then and there James and Sarah Moore started a family. They named the little girl Caroline. Who knows her real mother's name? Her mother, the gray woman, was taken care of too, reburied honorably. Nobody ever saw her again, neither. She must have known her child would be cared for with loving hands.

The gray woman had a pioneering spirit, for true. Let that be a testament about a mother's love for her child. A spirit sustained itself long enough to live only a short while yet strong enough to love forever, even with a broken heart. Some folks quit when it's a hard thing, give up the ghost, but she wouldn't.

History ain't nothing but stories of people, of a time and in a place. During the pioneering days of Carolina, the nameless Gray Woman lived her life and even lived her death. The plot where this story occurred lies somewhere with the many hundreds of submerged acres forming the basin of Lake Marion. There ain't no trace of the place today. All that's left of her history is her story.

I could only sigh and say, "Amen."

Note

There are many variants of this tale; America's frontier lore is full of such accounts. A premature burial was not uncommon before the sophisticated medicine practiced today. Also universal is a mother's protective love for her child. This tale incorporates both elements.

CHAPTER 9

Rx for a Best-Kept Secret

While waiting to fill a prescription at the pharmacy one day, I spotted the Lowcountry Liar shopping in the store. As usual, we got to talking, and he put his telltale sleight of hand to this ghostly story of Charleston.

Charleston has lots of stories about spirits and things that go bump in the night. They will give you thrills and chills, but they don't exactly end with "happily ever after" or some other etcetera. It's the nature of the beast.

Haven't you had the experience of being deep asleep in the quietest hour of the dark, dark night when, suddenly, you wake up? You're feeling so alone and can barely make out shapes of things you know are in the room. It's spoo-ky. Your hearing is tuned to every sound, the way a hound sniffs every scent on the trail.

Then you hear a noise.

It's subtle at first. It grows and becomes the only sound, except for maybe your heartbeat. You don't want to come face to face with the source, yet you feel you have to find out what the noise is. Where is it coming from? Nerve-racking is what it is.

Here in the Holy City, some say such spooky sounds come in several strains. Some swear they've heard the ghostly moaning and groaning of slaves bought in trade at the many dockside markets, or of the hanged pirates down along the Bat-tree and White Point Gardens, or of the Carolina colonials kept imprisoned in the basement of the Royal Exchange building during the Revolution. And that's not to mention murder and mayhem of the mundane-turned-mysterious kind. Even the old homes of Charleston, some from the seventeenth century, sing with creaks, cracks, and whispers. It's the city's history speaking up and peeking out. Witnesses to such acoustic nightmares have sometimes experienced a personal spiritual transformation.

One fella I know of here had himself a spiritual experience with something that went bump in the night. Andy McAdam lived downtown near the Bat-tree on Zigzag Alley. Andy and his wife, Fannie, lived comfortably in one of only four residences on the alley, a snug house painted as blue as the Carolina sky.

That's what we call "haint blue." You see, during the day, that bright sky-blue color keeps birds, wasps, and spiders from nesting, because it looks like the bright sunny sky above, and them critters appreciate some shade. But at night, during the witching hours, the haint blue is most beneficial, because it wards off evil spirits. The sky blue reminds them of Heaven above, and them things that go bump in the night want nothing to do with Heaven above. Many Lowcountry homes have haint-blue shutters and doors too—any access point of a household.

Andy and Fannie occupied the second floor of the little blue house. The house sat right where the zig of the doglegged little lane starts to zag. They could not be seen from the alley, but they could view who was coming and going below.

The landlord, Mr. McGrath, lived below but often traveled on business from Georgetown to Beaufort, so Andy and Fannie acted as homesteaders. Fannie diligently kept the household held together, while Andy did odd jobs maintaining the property as well as caretaking a few other lots belonging to Mr. McGrath. However, Andy's real vocation of choice was being an "entrepreneur in trade," as he called it. You see, Andy was a thief and a good one, well skilled in the dishonest occupation.

Andy's daddy, Joseph, had been a professional thief himself for more than forty years, but he got killed during a bank robbery. And his daddy, Andy's granddaddy Riley, had practiced his particular entrepreneurship during the haymaking days of postwar, Federally enforced Reconstruction. Riley allegedly was an elected official, but that must be only rumor, 'cause any such records have gone missing from city hall.

So it seemed that poor ol' Andy McAdam had been condemned

to continue the infamous family business. At night, he stalked the streets of Charleston, especially south of Broad Street. Our Broad Street is like Wall Street in New York City, a boulevard full of bankers and lawyers doing the business of guys in ties. We also recognize that Broad Street is a social wall separating everyone else from those who live South of Broad Street. All Charlestonians affectionately refer to these wealthy, discriminating denizens living *S*-outh *o*-f *B*-road *S*-treet as "S.O.B.S." It ain't no secret.

In that select neighborhood, Andy would ply his special entrepreneurial trade by raiding neglectful neighbors who left possessions unattended. Anything from a loaf of bread or last supper's leftovers to jewelry or the silverware could disappear if Andy dropped by. Naturally, it's kind of difficult to mind personal possessions in the dark of night when the business of most folks is to be sleeping soundly.

The unknown S.O.B. thief went about his nighttime networking, with nobody the wiser, although suspicious, that it might by Andy McAdam employed in the family trade. Andy's career as a sticky-finger vendor had kept his senses sharp, but his nerves had frayed over the years. There comes a time when even the best of the worst of us has to end his or her illegal activities.

The early-autumn evenings had turned cooler, so many neighbors habitually opened windows to invite nighttime sea breezes to slip through their homes like sweet lullabies. A typical Charleston single house is one room wide by two rooms long and gets pleasantly air conditioned when welcome currents of cool airflow pass through open windows at either end of the house. One soft September night, Andy happened to pass through Prices Alley, where the widow Eliza Manigault lived alone in a single house.

The widow, Ms. Liz to neighbors, had opened all her windows to ventilate, not thinking that might also be an unintentional invitation to unexpected company. In the Holy City, it's an open secret that "if the gate is open that is an invitation to visit." Well, Ms. Liz, for security, had locked the street-side greeting door to the piazza like a drawbridge gate preventing access to the property.

Andy had his thoughts wrapped around finding a suitable prospect for profit. From the front room of the widow's house, lights burned brightly into the darkness of Prices Alley. He noted shadows flickering across the walls of the room, so he stopped to investigate.

Andy snuck up to the nearest window. Standing in the dark on the steps to the piazza, he could watch Ms. Liz without being seen. He could eavesdrop easily.

Then he heard her.

"Oh, oh, oh, will it never stop? Night after night. Night after sleepless night. Oh, Alston, dear, it was never like this when you were alive. You always fixed things right. Oh, how I wish you were here now."

Andy was intrigued. Here was Ms. Liz talking to her dead husband, or maybe her dead husband's ghost! Andy kept listening to the widow by the window, marveling at her one-sided conversation. In her loneliness since the departing of her dear husband, Alston Beauregard Manigault, she just went on talking as if he were still listening to her.[1] Andy wondered if she sensed she wasn't alone.

Ms. Liz sounded so frightened, Andy thought. Her husband had been one of them high-grade S.O.B.S. Some say he had a stash of Confederate gold. Andy wondered if Ms. Liz knew of hidden treasure left by her husband. Could that be what she was fretting about? Was she wondering what to do with a possible fortune? Andy wouldn't mind suggesting a solution.

Ms. Liz went silent for a spell. Andy peeked into the room. She sat by the one door leading to the hallway but suddenly turned in her chair, leaning forward as if waiting a reply. Ducking down, Andy heard her get out of the chair. Slowly he rose up and stretched his neck, straining to hear something.

Then he heard it.

Ms. Liz heard it, too.

It was not loud but clear.

Tip-tap.

"Oh, Alston, make it stop! It's driving me mad. It's never ending!" She began to sob.

Andy remained rooted to his spot, rigid as a tombstone. He strained to hear it again.

Tip-tap.

Andy felt an uneasy, unpeaceful feeling creeping around his ribs. A silent wind rushed up, wrapped him in a wave of warm air, and then, as if by a switch, turned cool. Andy swallowed hard, his mouth suddenly dry. That strange sound seemed to be both there and not there.

Tip-tap.

"Oh, the *confounded tip-tap!*" wailed Ms. Liz. "Will it never cease? It's a curse!"

Tip-tap.

"Well, curse whoever hears it!" she half-shouted, half-screamed.

Hearing her say that, Andy felt faint. Could she hex him? He shook his head as if clearing it from a sucker punch. Cautiously looking around, he assured himself that only he and Ms. Liz were present, and, maybe, whatever was in the wind, a bump in the night.

Tip-tap.

Andy believed it best to leave. He stepped off the steps. *Creeeeak!*

"What's that?" Ms. Liz called out.

Andy fled.

"Who's there?" she cried.

By the time Ms. Liz came over, everything was still. She sighed and stepped away from the window.

Andy ran through the streets—crossing to Water, down brick-paved Church, turning seawards to Atlantic, and finally reaching Zigzag Alley. He took the steps three at a time up the staircase attached to the side of the house and burst through the doorway. Fannie nearly fell out of her rocking chair.

"Fannie, get up! I got to lie down. Help me!" Andy yelled, rushing into the bedroom, tearing off his clothes as he went. Fannie just stared, gap jawed.

"*Tip-tap, tip-tap,* that *confounded tip-tap!* I can still hear it," Andy muttered madly.

"Andy? Are you all right?" Fannie shouted as she stood up from the rocker.

"*Confounded!* Cur-sed! *Tip-tap!*"

"Andy? What are you talking about?"

"The *tip-tap!*"

Fannie hustled into the bedroom to find Andy in bed, gripping the sheets and covers at his neck with white-knuckled fists. She'd never seen him so scared. They'd both been frightened before, by fires, by hurricanes, by the threat of law enforcement, but this was something else.

"I'm cursed," Andy chattered. "I heard it. So, I'm cursed. If I see it, I'll die!"

"Andy, don't say such a thing!"

"Maybe it's not too late." He sat up in bed. "Fannie, dear, go fetch Dr. Ben."

Andy was in such a state of fright he seemed like a foreign country. Poor Fannie's spirits sagged under the untold weight of his mysterious misery. What mattered was the need of emergency help, so off she bustled to fetch the very good Dr. Ben.

Dr. Herbert Thaddeus Bennett currently held a head teaching position at the Medical University of South Carolina. Folks addressed him as Dr. Ben and he was widely respected, with a deserved reputation as both a sagacious teacher and a beneficent healer. He was known as someone who was always interested in the sundry shades of life. Dr. Ben also knew more than a little bit about natural botanical properties, most especially when human employment of the flora cooked up some of the local spiritualism. That's what's known as *hoodoo* or the Root. You might could say that ol' Herb knew herbs to a tee.

Fannie hurried over to Legare Street and luckily found the doctor at home but not yet abed. She was so flushed from running, and so flustered with alarum, that he could not deny her plea. Dr. Ben fetched his bag and followed Fannie back to Zigzag Alley.

There he was shocked at the sight of such a scared Andy McAdam staring back at him from the bed. Ghostly pale, Andy sat amid the sheets, twisting them in his agitation. His eyes stared wide, watching every corner of the brightly lit room.

"Andy. Andy!" Fannie firmly called. "Dr. Bennett's here. He's come to check you out, ok?"

"Andy, it's all right," the doctor said. "It's me, Dr. Ben. I brought my bag."

Andy blinked and seemed to come to. "It's a c-c-conjure,

Doc. The *tip-tap*. I'm cursed, Doc. I'm sure to die, maybe this very night!"

"Oh, now, Andy, don't be saying such and so," countered the doctor. "Tell me about this conjure you claim to have come across. Fannie says that all you'll tell her is this *tip-tap?* What about it?"

"I heard it; I felt it," Andy answered anxiously, beginning to perspire heavily. "Over to the Manigaults'. Ms. Liz was wailing about it."

Dr. Ben held Andy's wrist. "Well, tell me, did you speak with Mrs. Manigault?"

"I, uh," Andy started. He nearly misspoke. If he wasn't careful, he could expose himself as the S.O.B. thief. Andy explained, "I, uh, was passing by the Manigaults', uh, doing my usual evening neighborhood patrol. Yes suh, I patrol South of Broad, keep an eye out for any suspicious activity. Been a rash of thievery lately, you know?"

"Oh, yes, I know," said Dr. Ben. "This summer I had a burglary at my home."

"Oh, no, Doctor!" Fannie exclaimed. "What happened?"

"Well, I was giving a lecture at the university, but my wife was home. She was back in the kitchen, baking a cake and making tea. Someone rang at the front door, so my wife went and opened the front door but nobody was there. Then when she returned to the kitchen, nothing was there either. While she went to answer the front door, some culprit snuck around to the back and made off with everything."

"What all was taken?" Andy asked.

"Silver tea service, complete with sugar, milk, and hot tea, as well as a whole red velvet cake!"

"How mysterious," Fannie said. "How bold."

"Yes, it certainly was," agreed the doctor, glancing at Andy. "My wife still cannot believe such a thing could happen to her, in broad daylight. Thought she had imagined the whole thing."

"Well, I'm not imagining this," Andy averred. "The cur-sed, *confounded tip-tap* is gwine get me, Doc. I know it. I can feel it in my bones."

"All right, Andy, settle down. Tell you what. I'll go visit the widow Manigault, see what I can see—"

"She's cursed too, Doc, I swear. She heard the *tip-tap*. She got the curse," Andy warned. "Don't let her see you. You don't want to get hexed too, like her, like me."

"No, of course not," Dr. Ben assured him. "I'll be quiet as the proverbial grave."

Down the staircase and onto the street went the good doctor on his eavesdropping errand. He wondered about Andy's symptoms and story. He wondered about the widow and if she might be cursed. He wondered if there really was a ghost of a chance that Alston Beauregard Manigault himself had returned from the grave for his final dividend, whatever that might add up to.

Arriving at the widow's house, Dr. Ben cautiously positioned himself beneath the open street window closest to the piazza. No strange sound did he hear, but he could sense that someone stirred inside the house. Then he heard an eerie chant—

"Tip-tap, tip-tap, confounded tip-tap!"

It was Ms. Liz. Trying to hear better, Dr. Ben put his full weight on the piazza steps. *Creeeeak!* Ms. Liz flew to the window before the doctor could even think to hide.

"Who's there?" she demanded. The double barrels of a shotgun stuck out the window. Ms. Liz gave warning, "Either show yourself or get gone, and don't never return!"

The doctor froze in fear. The muzzle slid side to side across the windowsill. Dr. Ben swallowed hard and found his voice.

"Ms. Liz, uh, Ms. Eliza, ma'am. It's me, Dr. Bennett." He stepped away from the shadows to reveal himself in the streetlight. "See, I've brought my black bag." He held it up for her to see.

"Why, Dr. Bennett, what are you doing traipsing around in the dark like that? I didn't know you made house calls so late."

"Yes ma'am, I mean, no ma'am, ordinarily I don't. But I happened to be passing by." He didn't want to reveal his source on the matter. "Mrs. Manigault, I, uh, had concern for your welfare. As I walked by, and it's so quiet tonight, I heard you from the street."

"I don't need a doctor, Doctor."

"But the *tip-tap*, ma'am. I heard you. What about this *confounded tip-tap?*"

"What?" Ms. Liz asked, perplexed. "Dr. Bennett, are you a plumber, too?"

"Pardon?"

"Come on in, Dr. Ben. I'll show you to the hateful, *confounded tip-tap.*"

She let him in and led him through the narrow center hallway to the kitchen.

Tip-tap echoed clearly down the hall.

Tip-tap rang out loudly in the kitchen.

Tip-tap was right there in the room with them!

"There it is, Doctor," proclaimed Ms. Liz. "There is the *confounded tip-tap!*"

Dr. Ben followed her finger, pointing to the kitchen sink. He spotted a tiny drop of water beading up at the mouth of the cold-water faucet. It dripped into the sink . . . *tip-tap!* . . . *tip-tap!*

Turning so Ms. Liz couldn't see, Dr. Ben grinned like the Cheshire Cat.

"Well, Doc, what's your diagnosis? Think you can fix this jinx of a sink for me?"

Dr. Ben swallowed his smile, thinking about how best to answer her. It came to him in a flash: a cure-all for all his patients afflicted with a curse that night.

"Yes ma'am, I believe it'll all come out all right. Here's what we'll do. Come with me." He eased her nerves with a mild sedative, escorted her to bed, and bade her good night. By the time he returned to the McAdams' on Zigzag Alley, Dr. Ben had worked out the perfect prescription for his next pitiful patient.

The good doctor had decided not to let Andy know what he had found out about the faucet. Neither did Fannie need to know the whole truth. Certainly, Fannie knew more about Andy's activities than the doctor, but maybe she still didn't know everything about Andy. Sometimes people are best left in the dark.

When Andy and Fannie saw the doctor's worried face, they felt the end could be near. Fannie joined her hands together to pray. Andy rolled his eyes and let out a moan.

"Fannie, here's some sassafras root and leaves," Dr. Ben said as he rummaged in his black bag. "Do make us some tea, please, and let it steep good and strong."

Fannie, glad to have something to do other than fret, excused herself and went about the business of preparing tea. Dr. Ben sat down beside Andy, snapped his fingers, and waved a hand over Andy's eyes. Then he bent over him, bringing his face close to Andy's.

"Andy, Andy McAdam. Listen to me now, son. I can cure you of your confusion over this curse. This *confounded tip-tap.*"

Andy looked directly at Dr. Ben.

"You've got to trust me, Andy. You can keep a secret, can't you?"

Andy looked at him quizzically. "Doc, you know I can keep a secret. Come on, now. You do know how I make a living?"

"I have heard that you have a certain reputation, if that's what you mean. I also know that you McAdams have a family pedigree of renown."

"You mean my daddy, and granddaddy?"

"Yes, Andy, but more to the point at present, it's about yourself, your reputation. It's been said that a man's fate comes from his character, Andy. His character is his fate. It comes down to a kind of chicken and egg conundrum. Know what I mean?"

"I follow ya, Doc. I don't have no sack over my head."

"Good, good. But you know, Andy, no cure that I can prescribe will work fully without the patient also working with his own belief in the cure."

"Does that sassafras root got something to do with it?"

"Why, yes. It's a tonic and a strengthener. But you have to tonic yourself, Andy. Strengthen yourself against the former ways of your former family members. Turn over a new leaf. That's part of the cure, Andy. You will have to renounce your current, uh, occupation."

"Renounce my occupation? You mean give it up? Quit?"

"Yes."

"I don't know, Doc. It's in the blood. It's what I've been trained to do. To be."

"But it's not an honest trade, Andrew," Doc Ben said sternly. "Look, you have already proven that you, Andy, can be successful when you put your mind to it. You, Andy, know how to turn your hand to a task. Have faith, Andy, in yourself, and in the fact that whatever you choose to do, and do honestly, you can be successful at it."

"Tea is served!" Fannie cried, rolling in a finely filigreed teacart, on which she had arrayed an elegant silver tea service, replete with a pot of steaming hot tea, a cold sweating pitcher of fresh milk, and a covered sugar bowl with tiny tongs. Dr. Ben eyed the silver service. Andy eyed the doc. Neither of them spoke.

"Patients first," Fannie declared. She poured a simmering cup of sassafras tea, steam billowing, and sweetened it, making it altogether soothing. She handed the cup to Andy.

Andy sat silently as Fannie fixed tea for the doctor and herself. While they all sat sipping sassafras tea, Andy slowly unfolded his story. He acknowledged his family's infamous past, but balanced that by confessing to his own criminal faults. Fannie was surprised, somewhat. Dr. Ben sighed and smiled.

After the confidential, Dr. Ben gave Andy a promise.

"A promise for the future, to the future," Andy pledged. They shook on it.

That new future for Andy had appeared as bright as a new day to the good doctor when he stood in the kitchen of the widow Manigault. Dr. Ben realized with absolute certainty that there was no ghost at the Manigaults', only a leaky faucet. That's when he knew he could solve several problems with one solution, by prodding Andy to a new lease on life. If Andy could endure his own absolution, and turn over a new leaf, he could provide a service to his neighbors as well. But he had to leave off being a thief, forever and after.

Dr. Ben had told him, "Andy, you will hereby be pardoned from punishment, at least in this world. All is forgiven, no claim of resentment or vengeance. There will be no mention of our little secret tonight, and you shall be vindicated of any suspected crime or past criticism. Forget the ghosts of the past. It was all wind."

For a moment, Andy thought Doc Ben might hold a degree in law, or divinity, besides medicine. He certainly knew about wind. However, with some sane sense scared into him, Andy's newly declared faith in his future self wasn't wind.

It's long been said that there's no honor among thieves. Andy had promised to give up thieving to become an honorable man. His past became only a fading image, a mere memory when he believed that he had to steal anything of value. Being a thief in the night was no longer a satisfactory occupation. No longer did Andy suffer terrible torment from the *confounded tip-tap.* He wasn't cursed. He was cured.

There was a sudden lack of larceny South of Broad Street. Most folks believed that some band of thieves had stolen away into the night. Nobody knows to this day how Mrs. Bennett's tea service suddenly appeared at city hall.

After that fateful night, Andy proved good to his word, occupying himself with the daily pursuit of gainful employment by fixing anything his neighbors needed mended. And Andy found he liked the regular work, the fresh air and sunshine, and the sociable clientele. When he finished a round of repairs, there followed a round of recommendations for those who also needed a small deed done. Andy became an honest, hardworking handyman. He became known as "Handyman Andy."

In fact, one of the first jobs Andy handled was getting a grip on a leaky faucet tap in the kitchen of Ms. Liz, the widow Manigault. He was proud to fix it. She was happy with the end of the drip. It was a prescription for a best-kept secret—Dr. Ben's advice.

I told Jim, "That's one noodle-headed trickster's own-worst-enemy ghost story."
"It is that," Jim replied, nodding in agreement and adding, "tip-tap!"

Note

This odd little moral tale has its origins in India. It has an aural cue that demonstrates how we only hear what we choose to hear. The misinterpretation of the facts is followed by a threat of death, which leads instead to a happy recovery for all concerned. A possible moral to the story is: you will mend if you mind your own business. That's good medicine.

CHAPTER 10

The Return of "Rumpty Rattles"

The Lowcountry Liar is a licensed tour guide with the city, and one of the walking tours he offers is his Tavern Tales Tour. He poured out this frothy ghost tale about a different way to dance the Charleston during the Roaring Twenties.

I'm sitting in the Griffon pub at a window table, enjoying the view while noshing on a Reuben and a pint, when in walks my friend, the Lowcountry Liar himself, with a half-dozen folks following him. He waves to me as his group takes in the room, with its wall-to-wall and ceiling decor of stapled dollar bills, embellished and signed by patrons over the years. The group collects their drinks and sits at a table an arm's reach of me, so I lean over to say howdy to my friend.

"Hey, Jim, I was here the other evening and heard your name mentioned loudly by some fellas."

"Really? Do tell."

"Talked about your Tavern Tales Tour that they took. Raved about it."

"Well, glad they enjoyed the tour," Jim, responds, winking at his entourage.

"Sorry to interrupt the tour, folks, for some shameless promotion," I say. "Y'all are in for a real treat tonight if you're taking his tour. The two guys I just mentioned couldn't stop praising the good time they had, and they were locals, too."

"When did they say this?" Jim asks. I note an ever-so-slight smile slipping out.

"Let me see, this is Friday. That was . . . Monday? Yeah, just this Monday."

The tour troop tunes in to our conversation.

Jim casts a wide smile now, as though he has a shrimp net coming back full. "Oh yeah, I recall, two local boys down from Clemson on some break, had half a week off. Should be back up to school by now. Yeah, it was Sunday night we took the tour. We had a very special Sunday tour."

"Yes," I say. "They said it was a very special tour. Talked about visiting up the neck beyond the peninsula and the old city, to Magnolia Cemetery, right?"

"Well, yes, that's factual. Magnolia, and St. Lawrence, the Catholic cemetery right next door, they a bit up the neck, not down here where most of the ghost tours travel at night. But like I said, this was a special, Sunday special. I don't usually do pub walks on Sundays, but these fellas had recommendations from locals who were being tourists in their hometown, and as college kids like some y'all, they were curious, enthusiastic."

"So, off we go, like we did tonight about thirty-forty minutes ago. On that tour, besides me and these two Lowcountry bubbas, was a newlywed couple from L.A. That's not California, mind you. No suh, L.A. down here means Lower Alabama. The two lovebirds went, though they seemed distracted, a cozy crew of two. Like we did tonight, we all met down to the Market at Meeting Street to start the tour, then, as we did, crossed over to Beaufain Street, and that's when it really got started."

"What happened?" "What got started?" the tour troop asks, not unexpectedly.

"Well, now, y'all just heard me relate the tale about the sordid murder of one Frank Hogan, aka Rumpty Rattles. Truly a sad story of the bound-to-happen demise of a notorious bootlegger." Jim pauses and says, "How about we all raise a toast to the late, not much lamented Rumpty Rattles?"

So we do.

"Well, like I just told y'all a little while ago on that very same Beaufain Street, the site of the slaying, it was 1927. Charles Lindbergh was advancing aviation, flying solo across the Atlantic, and Al Capone was reaching out to everyone, becoming a royal racketeer. The date was October twenty-fifth; the clock had nearly ticked off the first of twenty-four hours. Like now, on the west corner stood the art-deco Riviera Theater, and to the east lay the Market. On the south side of Beaufain Street, with no streetlight, in an unoccupied building, by a shadowy window on the second floor, lingered one Leon Dunlap, erstwhile entrepreneurial partner with said Rumpty Rattles. Dunlap had with him a companion, one David Riggs, who also, recall, married the one-and-only daughter of said Rumpty Rattles. Rattles and Riggs were *related.*"

Jim pauses again and takes a quick sip of his drink. Half the glasses are raised, revealing varied rates of consumption.

"Nevertheless, the day before, Rumpty threatened the very lives of Riggs and Dunlap when with two other bootleg suppliers they had been making the rounds telling all the distributors that rates would be raised. They called on Rumpty at his home over to Blake Street, on his day off, which I guess even a gangster-bootlegger is entitled to. So, Rumpty's to home, and his wife's busy with her big soup cauldron on a constant boil in the backyard, neighbors and strangers waiting, ready for a ladle full. The Hogans had a community conscience, after all, kind of like a Robin Hood ideal."

Jim shakes his head.

"Calling the cops wasn't no charm in Charleston back in 1927. Leon Dunlap had known Rumpty Rattles a long while and knew not to cross him. Rumpty always seemed kind of rattled! Always carried what pirates and duelists called a brace of pistols. Two of a kind. That way, Rumpty could spare a gun for an opponent— his own updated take on the traditional duelin' code of honor. If not done exactly to the letter of the law, it was done in the spirit of the law. Can't say such benevolence in violence could counter the rotten-to-the-core soul of Rumpty Rattles. By any measured consideration, his only concern for the spirit of anything was for the booze he peddled. Cheers."

Again glasses raise and lower.

"So, between the time of calling on Rumpty at home and the first hour of the next day, Riggs and Dunlap patrolled the streets of Charleston with a newly purchased and loaded-in-the-interim twelve-gauge shotgun. They knew by habit that Rumpty would later likely drop by the Peking Chop Suey, a Chinese restaurant coincidentally by fate on Beaufain Street under a brightly lit streetlight, directly across from the afore-noted dark and derelict building."

Jim takes a long draw on his drink. He is savoring the taste as well as the rapt attention of his audience at the table. He is savoring the flavor of the narrator at work.

"All right, quiz time, college students," he says. "Any of y'all recall the why of Rumpty's arrival after midnight at the Peking Chop Suey Chinese Restaurant? Hands, please, ladies and gentlemen."

One of the cute coeds in the crowd chirps, "His girlfriend was getting off her shift then."

"A toast," Jim intones, "a toast to the miss with the correct answer. The girlfriend in question was Miss Myrtle Carter, the quintessential femme fatale. Rumpty shows up by one o'clock and walks to the entrance to cross the threshold into the aromas of the Orient and the arms of his lover. Instead, he gets thrust across the threshold of the forever after by Mr. Leon Dunlap. Most likely the next aroma Rumpty smelled was fiery brimstone." Jim smiles. "I don't know what that smells like myself, but for Rumpty Rattles, must have been something kee-yarn."

One of the coeds grimaces; another sticks out her tongue.

"Poor ol' Rumpty Rattles lay rumpled in a pool of his own blood, bleeding from more than a dozen wounds. He never had the chance to pull either of his pistols in defense. Dunlap calmly surrendered to the cops, handing over the shotgun like a prize. He and Riggs were tried for the outright murder in broad streetlight of an admittedly villainous denizen, and yet, they were acquitted on pleas of self-defense! O. J. Simpson has got nothing on Leon Dunlap. It was a clear-cut case of first-degree, premeditated elimination of the competition. Rumpty Rattles gave a new meaning to dancing in the street—dancing the Charleston, that is! Oh, man."

Drinks raise and lower all around. I have to ask. "What about Riggs and Dunlap?"

"Well, suh, one upshot of the shooting was that Riggs divorced Rumpty's daughter, even though both she and her mama, Rumpty's better half, sat with the defendants at the trial. Riggs returned to the country where he came from, a local yokel. Leon Dunlap spent a few years at a federal guesthouse for tax evasion, à la Al Capone. He later ran a legit restaurant establishment up the neck aways. Not too far from where he's buried. Which is—"

One of the lads in the group speaks up. "Was it Magnolia Cemetery?"

"Another elbow bend, everyone, for this young man with the correct-o answer! Yes suh, Leon Dunlap lies today in actual fact buried at Magnolia Cemetery."

Jim lets that hang in the air. He raises his glass to drink again but stops to say, "So does Frank Hogan, our Rumpty Rattles. Fewer than a hundred yards away." Jim swallows with satisfaction.

There is a collective gasp and a couple of "what?"s from the tour group.

Jim grins as if he's talking from a tree to Alice in Wonderland.

"Don't think I mentioned that particular fact earlier on the tour. Now recall, please, our two astute Clemson college students with whom I toured on Sunday. The day before, Saturday, the twenty-third, these two bubbas were at the Georgia Tech game in 'Death Valley.'[1] That's what alumni affectionately call the Clemson Tiger stadium. I don't doubt that they put the 'fun' in funeral, too.

"Anyway, the game didn't go so well for the Tigers after all, so our diehard duo figured by the time the ref whistle called the game, they could be pulling out of the parking lot. That's jus' what they did. They split from the stadium early, hit the road, and made a pit stop at Columbia halfway to here. Before they arrive in Charleston, these wily wizards of wisdom decide to slightly sidetrack over to Hell Hole Swamp to inquire about and acquire some Hell Hole Swamp Fire Water. Fine-as-wine shine. So, with a pint apiece, they cruise on home by about one in the a-and-m on Sunday, the twenty-fourth, a mere twenty-four hours in advance of the very eerie anniversary time of the shootin'."

No one drinks.

"That Sunday morning, the boys get hauled to church service, Charleston being a major source of leather in the Bible Belt, you know. There they meet up with three other ol' neighborhood bubbas, now Citadel cadets all in crisp uniforms, looking bright eyed and bushy tailed but kind of pi-qued around the gills. The night before, after the Citadel played host to Georgia Southern, these three cadets wound up on this very same tour that we're on tonight. It's a popular walk.

"Well, Saturday night on the tour, these three cadets stick together like the Three Musketeers. Likely later they invaded Big John's, a traditional Citadel hole in the wall, before making it back to barracks on campus. Wonder how that Sunday morning roll call come out, you know?"

On that cue, we all raise a uniform toast, as much of a military salute as we can muster.

"Apparently the cadets regale the Clemson comrades at church with stories of their riotous Saturday night and the Tavern Tales Tour, etc. Guess the impression burned deep. The dynamic duo, encouraged by the stalwart stories, just have to take the tour now, so that very night, as I said, off we go.

"These bubbas get so jazzed up on Rumpty Rattles that they keep talking about him throughout the tour. Keep in mind, they had been getting pretty jazzed up sipping that homebrewed joy juice during the whole tour. Most generous sharing the shine, too."

Jim winks at me.

"At Tommy Condon's, the Irish pub, after the last band break around midnight, we're standing on Church Street, couple of blocks from the infamous shooting site. There's about an hour till the anniversary. So, with such a rare occasion at hand, we just *had* to revisit the place, on time.

"We're standing on both sides of Beaufain Street when these two start playacting like it's the OK Corral shootout, the Wild West come East. It wasn't enough for them, though. That Hell Hole Swamp Fire Water stirred the inspiration in those good ol' boys. They come up with the brilliance born of bottled bravado to go out right then to Magnolia Cemetery to pay respects to Rumpty Rattles. And Leon Dunlap. It made sense then, given the conditions, and our condition. Hell, it still does to me."

A halfhearted toast ensues, no doubt out of respect for the words "cemetery" and "hell."

I intone, "Here, here!" Jim nods at me.

"Magnolia's an easy drive a couple of miles north up the neck, overlooking the *Coopa Riva*. We clamber into my car, a Taurus that I like to call 'the Bull Rider.' The drive up the neck to the cemetery seems to slide by as if we are swimming with the stream—something between flying and flowing. It's almost as if I'm not driving, only steering to our destination.

"We park at last, and by hook and by crook, we more or less quietly climb over the iron fence surrounding the cemetery and stand on hallowed ground. This was just a few days ago, about a week before Halloween, at the earliest hour of a Monday. We're half-drunk, with a half-pint of shine still. The moon peeps through clouds in the night air, heavy with graveyard silence. There's no telling what we may come to—or what may come to us—out there.

"As the tour guide, I orient us through the tombstones. I've been to Magnolia many times, looking up local history. Every stone there holds a story, and some of the stones are part of the same story, like tonight.

"I know that close by Leon Dunlap's grave, you can also find at rest John Bennett, the writer, a big voice in the Charleston Renaissance of the twenties and thirties. My favorite of his many works is his collection of Gullah ghost stories, *The Doctor to the Dead*. Bennett was a big influence on Lowcountry cultural life, like the hub of a wheel, with the spokes radiating outwards to different points, touching most everywhere. Like a guiding light, a polestar . . . but I digress.

"We don't talk as we walk the stone-garden pathways. Sound carries at such a time, in such a place. A cemetery at night ain't exactly fit for nonchalant chatter. Not to mention that our honorees were venal, vicious, sinful men committing more than mere venial sins.

"I guide us under the moonlight, and under a moonshine spell, to the John Bennett marker, where I bow briefly. Nearby we locate our outlaws, Leon Dunlap to the west and Frank Hogan, our Rumpty Rattles, to the east. At each site, we solemnly salute them with a swallow of Hell Hole Swamp Fire Water. To Rumpty Rattles! May he rattle nevermore!"

Once again the entourage raises a motley toast.

"You know, with names like Hogan and Dunlap, they had the makings of a suitable company name for any sensible business, but that was the crux of the problem: a sensible business. Rumpty Rattles never figured on that. He figured that he had it all figured out. And if not, so what? It only figures.

"By now, the life's about out of the party. I believe the tombstones sobered them boys up from the glow of moonshine. We climb out of the cemetery, and the ride back to town slowly unrolls us from the effects of, well, nearly everything. I say 'nearly' because by the time I deposit them back to the Market, they, no doubt inspired by intoxication, hatch a plan to perpetuate the night's occurrence.

"They figure to commemorate the anniversary of the involuntary, forced retirement of Rumpty Rattles. They get to suggesting a historic marker on the spot, a petition to the mayor to make the day an official city observance, a fan club, a Web site. I was so tickled, it was all I could do to focus on steering.

"So, in my capacity as a city-licensed tour guide, I designated Clem and his son, shall we say, to be the official planning committee for the forthcoming annual Rumpty Rattles Day. I figured I'd add a special restrictive instruction. You see, this particular committee can only meet to plan the festivities on the day before and the day after the anniversary."

Everyone laughs in relief. Several drain their glasses. I just shake my head.

"So, what you heard them boys talking about on Monday was the first ordained meeting to remember Rumpty Rattles." Jim downs his drink and looks at his entourage. "Y'all ready to travel? Got a great ghost story to tell y'all at the next stop."

I just shake my head. When they all get up to leave, Jim looks at me. I wink.

CHAPTER 11

The Setting of the *Rising Sun*

*Down at the Bat-tree on a blustery afternoon,
the Lowcountry Liar set the record straight about some early
Scottish emigrants who got the wind blown up their kilts.*

Labor Day afternoon, Jim Aisle and I were walking along the Ashley River on the west side of town. We strolled the Bat-tree from the Coast Guard Station to White Point Gardens, formerly known as Oyster Point, at the very tip of the peninsula. It didn't take Jim long to find a subject for a story.

"Now ain't that a crying shame?" he asked, waving his hand at the Ashley River.

"What?"

"There, see that hull sticking up some fifty feet out in the channel?"

"Uh, yeah, white with green trim?"

"Yep, that's it. Just the nose end sticking out the water."

"Water hazard, huh?"

"Ya think?" Jim cocked his head at me. "Just a mess. No way to care for a boat. Waste of a vessel and a hazard in the channel. Like roadkill in the highway."

"Wonder how many boats are bones out there, in the river or in the harbor."

"Well, we sank ships in the river channels to keep out the enemy, like the British during the Revolution, but the Redcoats surrounded us for six weeks. That siege was the only time Charleston ever surrendered. We did it differently during the War of Secession. Rather than plug up the waterways, we sank some of the Federal fleet, and we had a mortal ring of fire from forts guarding the harbor, too. The Yankees never got past Fort Sumter."

"*C'est la guerre,* as they say."

"Yep. Warfare. Only, war ain't never fair. It's all manmade madness."

"What about Mother Nature? Wonder how many ships have been sunk by hurricanes. Any idea?"

"No telling. Remember, we've been here since 1670, and not everyone's kept track. Besides, before they called them hurricanes, let alone started naming the 'canes, any sea storm was called 'dirty weather.'"

"Kind of generic. 'Dirty weather.' Covers a lot of lows and highs."

"Yes sir. The first major loss of a ship out here might have been back in 1700, during some of that—"

"Dirty weather?"

"That's right."

Jim paused and gazed across the water till I had to ask, "What happened?"

He looked at me from the corners of his eyes and raised his brows. "It's history. In fact, there's even a presidential connection. But it's a ghost story, too. You see, part of White Point Gardens has haints."

"It's haunted? Do tell," I said. I knew that Jim would launch into the story like a boat leaving its berth.

"Well, suh, you have to go back a little before 1700. Go back to Scotland."

"Scotland?"

"Yep. Back then, back there, some Scots thought they'd organize their own international trading company, like England had with the East India Trading Company, or the Dutch with the Royal Dutch Trading Company. All them companies were sort of national franchises. The homeland sent out manufactured goods, and colonies sent back tea, tobacco, indigo, hardwoods, silk, and such. The Scots East India Trading Company took a big chaw out of the tobacco trade to Europe."

"Uh huh. I see that every one of those imports you listed were exported from here in old Carolina."

"That's a fact, back when we were Charles Towne, an English colony. We sent out a slew of stuff. For instance, South Carolina's the only American colony to ever produce silk. Grew tea, too. Still grow tea on the only tea farm on the continent, out to Wadmalaw Island."

"So, Scotland was a player in world trade. Hmmmm. The more you look, the more you see, even if you're not really looking for it."

"Yep. The Scots also attempted to rival the English and Dutch and French and Spanish for New World territory, get some bragging rights. They planned a big settlement in the little, narrow Isthmus of Panama. They dreamed of capitalizing on the trade to and from the Atlantic and Pacific oceans. World maps by the 1690s showed the Isthmus of Panama having the least amount of land between the oceans. What could be simpler than to dig a little canal, from where you could control the trade between the oceans?

"But with all their planning, them Scots overlooked one wee little detail. The Spanish were right nearby already, in Colombia and Mexico. They'd been there a while, with fortified towns and all. They weren't too keen on having new neighbors. No doubt them Scottish bagpipes had something to do with it. The MacColonists called their settlement New Caledonia, or Darien, but it came to be known as the Darien Disaster."

"Uh oh, that doesn't sound good," I said. "A bit ironic, too, with the big dreams and big schemes. Remember, the great Scots poet Robbie Burns wrote, *'The best-laid schemes o' mice and men go oft awry.'*"

"Might say," Jim agreed. "That fella knew what he was talking about."

"What went wrong?"

"The English weren't too keen either on their sometimes unneighborly 'North Britons,' as they call the Scots, a-crowding in on the competition. That New Caledonia settlement might have led to a new war with Spain. Everyone in Europe was still licking their wounds from the last shooting match. Also, the English king back then, name of William, was really a Dutchman. It sounds a bit confusing, I know, but them royal power brokers often were more concerned with acquiring real estate to increase the real state they came from. Just like others now. Politics and power can be poison."

"Same old same old."

"For true. Anyway, King Billy pulled the plug on the funding for the project. So, the Scots had to finance the whole shebang, what with all the needed supplies, etc. That kind of cramped their style.

No self-respecting Scot likes to be in debt, and this setback put them in the hole, scrambling for new funding.

"Nobody knew wholly what they'd be getting into. Maybe they should have called off the whole thing, but they were eager beaver to beat everyone else at the colonizing game. National pride . . . national treasure . . . jealousy, I guess, as much as anything else—just the same old same old, as you said. That kind of focus can get you into deep, unredeemable trouble."

"Jealousy, that's one of the seven deadly sins, if I'm not mistaken."

"You ain't. It is. So is pride and greed. Them Scots, already envious of other maritime powers, now were mad as plaid about the expedition, and their bottom line. They finally collected enough collateral and sailed off for the New World, most all of them surviving the voyage. That ain't no small thing back in the days of sails and wind power. No suh, the biggest problem with the plan was the climate in the new land. That Isthmus of Panama's about as un-Scottish as the Sahara Desert."

"Tropical."

"But no paradise. Pestilential, more like. The heat, the humidity . . . Then add in the snakes and gators and other odd, New World critters. A dozen deadly dangers everywhere down there. Especially the mosquitoes—they were real popular, bringing everyone malaria and yellow fever."

"Same as here, initially."

"Yes suh. But it's gotten better. The Scots were only used to wet forty-degree weather, wool clothing, heather-covered hills, oatmeal. They began dropping like—"

"Flies?"

"No, I was going to say rain, like the raindrops of the rainforest. The Caledonia colonists were as busy building coffins, digging holes, and burying their kin as they were trying to construct a settlement. Plus, the Indians in the bush scared them somewhat, though the natives mostly kept at a distance. Plus another minus, the Spanish had coastal forts nearby and kept harassing the Scots, as bad as mosquitoes.

"At the last, too many of them were too sick, and too few were able to resist the Spanish. So they come to an accord. Those Scots still standing piled their household goods onto their ships, the cannons and all, and set sail for home. But timing is everything. It seems the New Caledonia expedition was doomed from the get-go."

"A fatal forecast, eh? It sounds like the luck of the Irish."

"Well, they are Celtic cousins. Scots or Irish, generally their history has included strife, warfare, starvation, eviction, forced migration. Some luck! So it seems them Scots got some of that Irish luck. Despite it all, they were devout, churchgoing, God-fearing Presbyterians, folks with a deep belief in what they call predestination. Kind of fatalistic, but not really pessimistic. Mostly mystic, I guess. It's about being chosen, pr-determined. Well, suh, determined they definitely were, whatever their sins.

"And as you mentioned the seven deadly sins, you know we call them that because they might make you dead. There's anger and lust, greed and gluttony, envy and pride, and sloth. It's odd that a sloth is a tree-hanging critter from the rainforest, right where them Scots had been. The deadly sins can dovetail on each other; anyone can be guilty of more than one at the same time. I'm not saying the Scots had devilish designs. But they had been distilling a deadly sin cocktail by mixing pride, envy, greed, etcetera. Add in some Irish luck for spice, or maybe for spite? Set the brew on the back burner to boil, and it'll serve up deadly enough."

"How did they wind up here in Charleston?"

"They left the isthmus after thirteen months—and ain't that a lucky, prophetic, determination of fate? They departed Darien in April with five ships but lost one ship crossing to Cuba and another when trying to dock it. The surviving three ships sailed on, the *Duke of Hamilton*, the *Speedy Return*, and the *Rising Sun*. Off the Florida coast, they got caught in a hurricane, some of that nasty dirty weather. It hit them so hard that the *Rising Sun* lost all her masts, and the repairs delayed them. It took four months to reach Charleston from Darien. It took them less time than that to cross from Britain to the Isthmus in the first place.

"By August, they were riding anchor outside Charleston harbor, the ships too big and heavy to cross the long, large sandbar at the harbor's mouth. Not that visiting the city then would have been advisable. We had been having a run of some of that notorious Irish luck ourselves, for three years in a row."

"And luck, good or bad, often comes in threes," I added.

"It do. Before the hapless Scots showed up, Charlestonians suffered a smallpox epidemic during 1697, lasting from summer into winter the next year. It killed hundreds of settlers and slaves and maybe thousands from local Indian tribes. Following that, in early February 1699, came an earthquake, a-rattling every building as well as everyone's last nerve. Following that, a week or so later, a fire raged for two days, burning down a third of the town and leaving fifty families homeless. Following that—had enough yet—came a worse-than-usual outbreak of yellow fever that wiped out another couple of hundred victims. It was an epidemic by the time the Darien Scots showed up.

"Aboard the *Rising Sun* was one Rev. Archibald Stobo, a well-known name to the Presbyterian settlers here. They invited him to come preach that Sunday at the Independent Meeting House. That's where the Circular Congregational Church stands now, still in covenant with the Presbyterian Church. I guess it been predestined that they be there forever.

"A Lieutenant Graham and a dozen oarsmen, all from the ship, carried the preacher and his wife over to shore. Upon request, Reverend Stobo had come to supply the good word afresh to the local congregation. Under orders, Lieutenant Graham had come to request fresh supplies for the good colonists cooped up on the *Rising Sun*. The service was given, supplicant prayers said, and some food and clean water obtained. The next day, right when they were ready to return to the *Rising Sun*, all hell broke loose."

"Dirty weather?"

"Dirty, and dark as death. Swirling winds and surging tides swept over the coast, creating havoc for the inhabitants on shore and especially aboard ship. While we lost some wharves to the waves, the *Rising Sun* again lost all her masts to the wind, in just a matter of minutes. The ship pitched in the furious fit of the storm, rolling from port to starboard, rocking from stem to stern.

"The wild weather smashed into the ship unchecked and unadulterated, as pure terror struck the hearts of every soul aboard. Overloaded with cannons and housewares, the *Rising Sun* listed to portside when the weight shifted. Unrelenting pressure from the sea split the timbers of the hull, and water poured in below and washed the decks above. Bashed repeatedly against the bar, the ship began to break up. The *Rising Sun* would soon be setting, for true.

"No one aboard survived the storm. Not one Scot. The only souls saved were the fifteen who had come ashore. Searching for days after, Lieutenant Graham and his squad, led by locals, recovered ninety-seven bodies from James Island. Reverend Stobo blessed them all. They buried them out to Coffin Island, hence the name, except now it's Folly Island, the Edge of America. Well, suh, folly brought them Scots to a sandy coffin."

"But Jim, if they're buried on Folly, how did White Point Gardens become haunted?"

"Like I said, no one aboard the *Rising Sun* survived when it broke up. But not all the passengers were aboard. The ship's passenger list totaled 112, besides the crew of thirteen, who were all ashore with Reverend Stobo and his wife. So the count was 110. Only 97 were found. That leaves a lucky group of thirteen unaccounted for."

"You know what happened to them?"

Jim stopped and spread out his arms to indicate the Bat-tree before us. Walking and talking, we had arrived at White Point Gardens. We stood by the seawall at a spot that bisected the park.

"As legends go, I can tell you what fate befell them Scots, where they lie today, why this very stretch of shoreline's haunted. Just before the *Rising Sun* sank, one family clan clambered into a lifeboat and launched themselves into the sea. Waves carried the light craft over the bar and up the Ashley River. From that side of the sandbar, on James Island not far off, stood the Johnson Point Watch Tower, a prototype lighthouse. The courageous clan figured to make for the Point and beach the boat. Only, the wind was too strong and the waves wouldn't cooperate. They shot on past the Point, farther up the Ashley.

"The next best landfall was Oyster Point, rye-cheer, the White

Point Gardens. Again figuring to beach the boat, straining every muscle trying to steer through the channel, and praying with every thought for guided deliverance, the clan of thirteen clung on till the last hope. They nearly made it too, but the elements were overwhelming. They boat capsized; couldn't have been but a couple of dozen yards out. It ended up where we're standing now. Everyone drowned.

"The *Rising Sun* had been bashed, smashed, crashed. The lifeboat had been swamped, dunk, sunk. The bodies had been beaten up on the rocks, shredded by the shells. They weren't much to look at but plenty to eat for the crabs and gulls."

"Ugh. Who were they? You mentioned a clan."

"Clan Craig. Three married couples, two adult males, four children, an infant. They're all included on the passenger lists from Panama, but they were unaccounted for at the end of the voyage. It's believed they hailed from Aberdeen. It's a really ironic name, what with all they suffered. "Craig" means rock, a crag. They had a rocky voyage from the rocky colony, and they wound up on the rocks. I don't know if I ought to consider that to be predetermined, like doctrine. Decide for yourself if it's divine interference."

"Retribution? Redemption? Punishment for the seven deadly sins?"

"Only God knows. All I know is that the bodies washed up to what's now this garden park, from Church to Meeting to King streets. That's furthermore ironic. Those names kind of mock the victims. The Craigs gathered up, congregating like at church for a meeting with the king. We can only hope they were pardoned by the Almighty."

"But wait, earlier you mentioned something about a presidential connection. Who? How?"

"More irony, for true. Predestiny. Remember how the mosquitoes ate on them Scots, delivering yellow fever, causing calamity? And Reverend Stobo? He spent the rest of his days in Carolina, causing his own chaos with the English authorities in the colony. Well, suh, skip on down six generations to one of his descendants, through the Bulloch clan of Georgia. Miss Martha Bulloch married a Mr. Theodore Roosevelt of New York. They had a son, Teddy Jr., who

became the twenty-sixth president of the U.S.A., 200 years after the good Reverend Stobo stopped off ashore to give a Sunday sermon.
"This is the kicker. Theodore Roosevelt, Jr., became the American president who led us to build the Panama Canal across the isthmus. He accomplished in spades what his Scots ancestors had only hinted at in their futile attempt. Because of the rampant yellow fever down there, Dr. Walter Reed would develop a vaccine to protect against the deadly disease. As an example, Havana, Cuba had some twenty thousand cases of yellow fever at the turn of the century, but only two years later, not a single case was reported across the entire island! They named a hospital up to D.C. for the good doctor."

"Wow. Amazing how all that can connect to Charleston, and in such a strange way. Still, you say only this stretch of the Bat-tree is haunted? How far does the haunting extend?"

"Roughly, it's between Church, Meeting, and King. On one end, you have the Fort Sumter Hotel at King Street. On the other end, East Bay Street runs along the Coopa Riva to form the corner of the High and Low bat-trees. Used to be a public bathhouse there. Before the hotel were wharves on the river. But nothing has ever been built on the shore from the bathhouse to the wharves, right where the clan Craig lay, unsung victims of the *Rising Sun*.

"I've been down here *fushing*, crabbing, *shrumping*, what have you, from evenings to the early-morning hours. Sometimes, I've felt a feeling, a presence not seen, a vibe. I've heard strange moaning and groaning. I can't translate it, only place it rye-cheer, where nothing ever was built. Coincidence? Over the many years since the sinking of the *Rising Sun*, it's been said, because they've been heard, that the mournful sounds from those lost Scottish souls still call through the ages. They were never buried or blessed. The Craigs were so close to shore, so close to salvation, yet never found a safe haven, perhaps not even in heaven above. They still echo in the quiet of the night at White Point Gardens."

I sighed. Jim added, "Might say the Point won't never be Scot-free."

Note

The hurricane season is an annual reminder that Mother Nature can be fickle. Fate can be too. History proves itself to be a series of facts and acts that leave tracks, or maybe not.

The drowned bodies from the *Rising Sun* washed ashore along James, Morris, and Folly islands. Some on the passenger list were never recovered. This story is a plausible account why, like any ghost story.

The Anglicans were the power elite and the predominant faith in colonial Charleston. Their primary house of worship was—and some say still is—St. Philip's Episcopal Church, the oldest such congregation south of Virginia. The church is located on Church Street, which is how the street got its name. Non-Anglican Protestants were called Dissenters collectively and included Scots Presbyterians. Dissenter sects shared a building for their services, which was not recognized as a church but a "meeting house." The site sits on Meeting Street, which is how the main street of Charleston derived its name. Over the centuries, there have been four meeting houses there, each rebuilt after being destroyed by fire or earthquake. Meeting Street has always been pronounced with the final *g,* even by native Charlestonians. That does not prevent you from attendin' a meetin' on Meeting Street.

Oyster Point, or now White Point Gardens, is the name for the tip of Charleston's peninsula, where the Ashley and Cooper rivers meet at the Atlantic Ocean. The English colonists named the point when they first arrived in April 1670. Native tribes had for generations discarded oyster shells there after harvesting the meat, so it became an archaeological midden, or natural garbage dump. The sun reflected blindingly off the white shells, making it a ready-made landmark for mariners—a sort of horizontal lighthouse.

The Wadmalaw Tea Farm conducts public tours and is a fascinating visit.

PART III: THE MOOGLY

CHAPTER 12

A Cure for What Ails You

One evening standing by the cemetery of the Circular Congregational Church, the Lowcountry Liar unearthed this remedy for the things that go bump in the night.

Sammy Prioleau lived his life peaceably down around Meggett, South Carolina. Meggett's a quiet little rural town, fresh-air clean. You pass it on your way from Charleston to Edisto Island. Living there is just as easy as it is anywhere else in the Lowcountry.

Sammy worked as a deliveryman for a furniture store during the week and did odd jobs on weekends, whatever he could to make money. He amassed a sizeable bundle of disposable income; Sammy wasn't one to squander. During winter, spring, and summer, he saved up for a special night on the town. In the fall, he would visit Charleston when the MOJA African Arts Festival got under way, an annual event celebrating the Sea Island culture of the Lowcountry. Sammy had something to spend his money on now.

On a Saturday late in September, Sammy folded his surplus bills into a wad of wealth and dressed in a set of Sunday clothes. He didn't drive so had arranged a ride with a couple of guys to downtown Charleston. They dropped Sammy off at the Market since they had things to do elsewhere. Sammy stood by a little cat alley where they all agreed to meet later, as they said, "back at the ranch." As they drove off, Sammy happened to look down the cat alley and noticed a big red barn at the other end where carriage tour rides were offered, a good landmark.

Sammy walked down to the customs house for the block party, enjoying the festivities immensely, digging it all. He watched, listened, and swayed along with colorfully costumed dancers strutting their stuff. He joined in a drum circle, literally lending a hand to the band. He spent money sampling snacks, such as boiled peanuts and benne-seed wafers, and buying a couple of colorful shirts from the vendors.[1] He rode the trolley up to Hampton Park for some main events.[2]

Oh, he was having a high time, for true. Late in the day, Sammy's stomach growled loudly, repeatedly, for more substantial food, and he decided the funnel cake and corndog fare wasn't fair enough. He decided to entertain himself with some of Charleston's renowned cuisine. So he caught the trolley back to the Market, with its array of restaurants among the vendors and retail shops.

Sammy couldn't select which one restaurant to haunt, there were so many to choose from. Besides, with such a wide variety of dishes offered everywhere, he couldn't settle on any particular fare anywhere. So Sammy came up with a compromise. Instead of enjoying a full-course main meal on his plate at one place, he would order only appetizers at each and every restaurant in the Market. A smorgasbord, you know?

Sammy crisscrossed North and South Market streets, showing his shadow at every eatery. He downed cheese sticks, baby-back riblets, fajitas topped with sour cream, fried shrimp, boiled shrimp, jumbo shrimp and grits, popcorn shrimp, oysters on the shell and off the shell, barbecued pulled pork with both mustard sauce and vinegar sauce, half a dozen eggrolls, and a batch of Vidalia onion rings with horseradish sauce. He drank a beer or two with his menu, too, but mostly drank sweet tea or ice water to cool off his palate. Finally, at the Olde Fashioned ice-cream parlor, he added a double scoop of rocky road ice cream on a cinnamon waffle cone. Yes sir, sweetness and spice are the very variety of life. Of course, in the course of ingesting all the courses, Sammy perhaps invoked a culinary curse. You are what you eat.

By now, it was very early Sunday morning, the crowds were thinning after the last rounds, and Sammy realized he needed to be headed home at last. He headed "back to the ranch" to meet up with his ride. He located the big red barn and looked in every direction, but no one ever showed. Sammy had missed his ride home; the other fellas, if they hadn't forgotten him, probably got tired of waiting. Now Sammy was stranded.

Unfortunately, his options were limited, because his funds had diminished. A cab would cost way out of the way too much, more than he had on him, and it would come close to twenty miles to hike home to Meggett. It was too late to get a room, though he'd only need one for a few hours. Anyway, all the hotels were booked for the festival. Downtown is expensive, and Sammy had not budgeted to cover the cost of renting a room. Cheaper motels would be on the outskirts of town, but they were still a hike away.

What should I do? Sammy wondered as he wandered the Market. Ambling down Church Street, he happened to pass St. Philip's Church. He stopped to stare up at the steeple. Sammy contemplated his plight, right there by the parish graveyard, a quiet, peaceful, restful resting place, as it should be.

Sammy snapped his fingers. Why not spend the night in St. Philip's graveyard? Scattered throughout the cemetery, like rectangular rock islands amid the funereal sea, stood raised tombs—stone tabletop cases of rest. He figured he could stretch out on one like a bed, so long as he could keep his mind off what lay beneath the stone pillow. Who would be the wiser? What would be the harm?

Sammy scanned the street for any other pedestrians. No one was looking around but him. So Sammy scrambled over the iron fence of the graveyard. The black metal bars felt cold as ice, odd for late September, but he dismissed the discomfort, instead minding the spikes on the top of the fence. He searched for a suitable tomb to embed himself upon. He didn't want to be seen from the street, but he wished to have the security of the streetlight as a nightlight. He finally found a fitting place, climbed on top, and curled up as comfortably as possible for slumber. In no time Sammy was snoring, sawing logs.

An hour later, Sammy suddenly woke up. He yawned and belched, but it wasn't indigestion that woke him up. It was something else, in the graveyard. He listened intently but heard only the wind shaking bare branches like rattling bones, a melancholy sound. Peeking round, he saw no one else present, not even a stray cat. Slowly Sammy closed his sleepy eyes again.

Then again, minutes later, something made him open his eyes. This time Sammy surely heard it. *Thump! Thump!* It was very faint at first, but then more distinct. *Thump! Thump!* What was it?

The sound came from behind him. Sammy shifted to look over his shoulder. He stared into the dark shadows of the graveyard . . . but saw nothing. He couldn't distinguish anything other than tombstones, shrubbery, shadows.

Then, he clearly heard it again. *Thump! Thump!* There followed a rough scraping sound of . . . maybe something heavy sliding over the ground. Sammy peered into the darkness and saw it. It was a coffin, climbing out of a freshly dug grave!

The oblong box raised up at an angle halfway out of the hole and *whump!* It landed flat, up on the lawn. Slowly the coffin turned to Sammy, who sat dead still atop the tomb.

Speechless, not that calling for help would help, Sammy eyeballed that box. The coffin started sliding over the lawn towards him, then bumped against the tomb he sat on. Sammy climbed off the other side. The coffin turned and came around the tomb. Sammy backed away. The dark box followed him every which way he went, left or right, step for step, across the graveyard.

At the iron fence, Sammy quickly climbed up and dropped over, safe on the street. But the coffin jerked upright, slid up the graveside of the fence, and teetered on the top of the spiked metal bars. Then it slid down onto the sidewalk.

Sammy shivered, but he wasn't cold, he was scared. He ran down the street, not caring where to, just away from that coffin. He didn't know where to go, where to hide. At this early hour—a time for haints—there was no one else on the streets, only him.

Him and that coffin, that is. Sammy ran off, but that coffin followed him, sliding with a skin-crawling scraping sound on the pavement. He ran up Church Street to Market Street. He found Meeting Street, the main drag through peninsular Charleston, but that coffin kept right behind his every step.

Sammy ran up Meeting Street for a few blocks, then cut the block over to King Street, another long avenue. That confounded coffin tailed him. Not a single pedestrian did he pass, not even a lonesome cab or any other traffic. This time of night, hag-hollerin' time, is when mysterious things that go bump in the night come out to go bump in the night!

Sammy doubled back towards the Market. He remembered seeing an all-night minimart in the neighborhood. Maybe there he could find sanctuary. The coffin hounded his heels as he hightailed his way down the silent streets. His lungs burned; he was running out of breath. His throat ached and throbbed, even though he had been too scared to scream. His whole body felt feverish.

Rounding the corner at Cumberland Street, Sammy saw the store with the Open sign lit up. He pushed himself with a last-ditch effort to reach safety. As Sammy yanked open the door, the jolly jingle bell overhead clanged in alarm, and the clerk behind the counter half-jumped out of his chair.

The coffin followed in before the door closed fully, wedging itself in the doorway and then crossing the threshold. The door shut behind it with a sudden sharp jingle, and the coffin was inside. Sammy was trapped.

Sammy stared at the oblong box, dumbstruck. The clerk fainted. Sammy backed down an aisle. The coffin came on again. Looking left and right for any saving grace, Sammy frantically started throwing bags of chips, candy bars—anything he could grab—at that coffin, all to no avail. It kept coming, getting closer, closer, closer. There was no place left to go for poor Sammy.

Suddenly, the coffin rose up tall on one end. It rocked back and forth, inching forward. The lid began to open.

Desperately, Sammy reached out to a shelf and snatched up the first thing that came to hand. It was a bag of mentholated cough drops.

Sammy stared at the bag and noticed that each medicated drop was individually wrapped. It was on sale, too. Without another thought, Sammy reared back and pitched the bag of cough drops at the horrible oblong box.

And . . .

What happened next?

Don't you know? Sammy finally *stopped that coffin!*

After a pause, the Lowcountry Liar added, "Now that's a dead end, for true!"

Note

Some stories tell themselves. This story builds to a frightful climax, then lets you have it, right between the eyes. This type of tale truly begins as "Once a pun a time . . ." There is a groaner of a punch line at the end. It may, or may not, leave you feeling "happily ever after." However, you will want to tell it to someone else.

CHAPTER 13

The Headless Horse Ma'am

There's enough trepidation incurred when shopping for a new car, and one time the Lowcountry Liar had to go along for a hair-raising ride in the bargain.

This is as true a tale as I can tell you. I went down to the Ford place on Savannah Highway one Saturday afternoon in late October to maybe buy a new car. I thought a Taurus might do me just fine. I didn't want no SUV. That would be overkill for me, and none of them had a price under what I planned to spend. I didn't need a truck, since I live on a boat, the *Coota*.[1] No, I wanted something more sporty, something sedan sized, and the Ford Taurus seemed to be right in the range. The name *Taurus* was a bonus. If you know the zodiac signs, that's the bull, and what better sign is there for a bull-slinger like me?

So I selected a car off the lot, sandy gold with a tan interior. I didn't want too dark or too light a color. A salesman rode along shotgun, so he could shoot off to me about all the beneficial attributes of the latest Ford factory creation. Standard car-salesman spiel, you know the drill.

It turned out that the salesman, Chuck, was originally from Chillicothe, Ohio. He seemed kind of nervous, maybe anxious to make a sale. To set him at ease, I told him that me driving and him being from Ohio made me remember when I took a driver's-ed course back in high school. We had to watch some horrendous films of actual car wrecks, with hideous human remains strewn all over the highway and splashed on the screen. It was ghastly, man. Human body parts were displayed like no anatomy class would show. Some students got ill watching the gore. Every one of them instructional films had been shot and produced in Ohio by the highway patrol. I learned to drive just fine and passed the class, but what else I learned from them films was that I don't never want to drive in Ohio. Chuck winced a smile.

So we were tooling down Wappoo Road when we came to where it crosses Ashley River Road, beehive-busy Highway 61.[2] It was late afternoon, when most all the intersections get crowded, especially on day-off Saturday. We were only doing thirty, thirty-five tops, through the business neighborhoods, and I sure didn't want to have to sit in traffic for a test drive. I was thinking how I'd like to open it up, get on the interstate, use the cruise control, get real sporty, you know? We had a couple of options to make the interstate from Highway 61, but either way had *way* too many traffic lights to stop and go through before we could ride the wind. So, compromising instead, we stayed on 61, sliding up towards Summerville along the backdoor hurricane-evacuation route.

Next thing, we were rolling on Ashley River Road headed out of town. Once we got past one last traffic light, we were on a fine stretch of treelined, two-lane blacktop for many miles running roughly parallel to the Ashley River towards Summerville. We passed the historical sites of Drayton Hall, Magnolia Gardens, Middleton Place Plantation, all registered landmarks of the colonial era. I figured I'd play tour guide on this test drive. I could chat up Chuck, put him more at ease.

On either side of the road, tall oak trees stretched their long gnarly limbs overhead, all draped in Spanish moss. We cruised by the historical sites—well, past the signs for them anyway, since they can't really be seen from the road; they're all down by the river. Chuck was liking the view all the same. I suppose he expected to see Capt. Rhett Butler and Miss Scarlett appear like ghosts in the wind.

We were having a fine afternoon drive, so we kept on. There was hardly a soul else on the road in either direction, so I guessed right about the traffic. I mashed down on the accelerator, put some juice in the blender.

We were halfway to Summerville and the daylight was starting to fade before I agreed to head back. It was getting on towards suppertime, anyway. I pulled over and set up to make a U-turn, waiting for a lone pickup to pass by in the other direction. I was watching it, timing my turn, when I saw something strange. Or, I didn't see it, actually. It was an odd sight, anyway you look at it. I thought I saw something that wasn't there, and it should have been.

There was no driver in that pickup truck!

At first, I disbelieved it. I pulled out behind the truck, and as we followed it back to Charleston, I decided to find out for sure. I zoomed up, tailgating tight. The truck was all black with chrome highlights, bumpers, door handles, and window frames. It had *Dodge Ram* stamped in silver on the tailgate, with an embossed silver head of a ram in the middle. That little ram face looked kind of ornery, and I bet if it had eyes they'd never blink. But it wasn't just the shiny chrome and the blackness of the truck that seemed sort of ominous; the windows were tinted and only reflected the shadows of the trees it passed by. I couldn't see who was driving this rig, and it was one big, high-chassis pick-em-up, too. From behind, it looked as if nobody was in the cab at all—no driver at the wheel, no shotgun rider, not a soul. It was just a big shiny black mobile machine rolling down Ashley River Road with Chuck and me in tow.

I shared my observations with Chuck, which made him sit up a little bit straighter. He pulled at his seatbelt and adjusted himself. I wasn't too sure, but I thought he crossed himself too.

I told him I'd pass the truck as soon as the yellow divider lines and any oncoming traffic allowed. I told him to scootch himself up to peer into that cab as we passed the driver's side to see if he could see the driver. I told him to hang on tight; this might be a hell of a ride. He turned to me and I saw he didn't look at ease, but he was game.

Soon enough we were passing the Ram. Chuck unbuckled, lowered his window, stood up as much as he could, and stuck his head out the window as we rode past. He was eyeballing the cab, looking for a human inhabitant, till I pulled in front of the truck and Chuck full collapsed in his seat like a pile of laundry.

His face was bleached as white as a sun-dried bed sheet on the line. He didn't speak but kind of leaked like an accordion, breathing heavy in little pitiful pant, pant, pants. He had asthma maybe. I finally had to ask him, "Well?"

He slowly turned to me, shaking his head back and forth, all solemn like. He blinked a few times, swallowed hard, and got his breath at last. Finally he said, "I couldn't tell. I couldn't see a head!"

My eyes went wide. I was getting kind of spooked. Granted, as a yarn spinner, I've told some tall ones, and I've heard some tales too, vouched as gospel, but this was a bona-fide experience, for true. We both got the jitters now. I looked at Chuck for a long minute till I nearly ran us off the road. It gave me a bad flashback of them Ohio road-kill films.

"You sure you didn't see nothin'?" I asked him. "Nobody? Nothin'?"

"N-no. No one. I think I might have made out a tiny pair of hands gripping the steering wheel. That's all. I'm not sure."

I looked in the rearview mirror. I guess while we talked I slowed down without thinking, because that big black Ram now looked to be charging to catch up to us. I don't know if the driver, or whowhatever, didn't like to be passed, but I planned not to linger for any sort of explanation. We shot off.

The daylight was faded out now and I knew the haints would soon be out roaming for souls. That's when it's too late, ain't no going back. Suddenly the black truck flashed its headlights, all but blinding us. The lights flashed two, three, five times. I didn't know if it wanted to pass, or eat us alive.

It was like some kind of driving dance with us and that black Ram. It closed on our rear bumper, backed off, closed again, no matter our speed. We still couldn't see no driver. Poor Chuck looked as if he might live *up* to his name, if you know what I mean. There we went, chased down Ashley River Road during dusk with a headless driver in a night-black Ram pick-em-up truck. It made me recollect that tale with the headless horseman, and I also recollected the less-than-happy ending to that chase.

Like that Ichabod fella from the story, we craned our necks, looking for an escape route, but we came up with a goose egg. There was nothing but a two-lane blacktop highway hemmed in by darkening woods. We half-expected a flaming pumpkin any second.

Chuck slumped in his seat. He was speechless, no doubt all dry mouth, but sweating as though he was in a sauna. I wasn't sure if he was trying to set on his knees to pray but the dashboard was in the way. He was making himself into a pretzel, twisting around to see what was what behind us.

"No, don't look into the lights!" I shouted, but it was too late. Chuck whipped back round, blinking as if he was sending semaphore signals. The truck lights flashed a couple of more times, urgent, angry like.

"Make them stop," Chuck pleaded.

Only then I realized that I hadn't put on my beams yet, so I switched them on. Chuck saw the lights come on in front of us and looked at me as if to say, "Why didn't we think of that?" Feeling sheepish, I just shrugged.

And I sped up. That truck was still stuck to our tail. It was evermore bearing down on us. The lights weren't flashing no more, but they glared as if it was Judgment Day.

Back to town we raced, passing Middleton Place, Drayton Hall, and a whole slew of churches on both sides of the road: Baptist, Methodist, AME, Episcopalian, Presbyterian, you name it, but there wasn't no saving grace from any of them, since none of them would open for business till the next morning. By then it would be too late for Chuck and me. There would only be mourning in the morning.

We passed the Live Oak Memorial stone garden, with its proud sign for *perpetual care* boldly showing, only I didn't care to be perpetually resting yet. No sir, and there ain't nothing like a graveyard to spur you on. I put a spur to the horsepower right then.

It didn't matter. We would be road-kill if I couldn't outdrive this fiend in the machine behind us. That big Dodge Ram was making like to ram us clean into eternity.

Then I sighted the Cross Creek Bridge. Hallelujah! No haint worth damnation can cross moving water, and we were moving hell-bent for leather. I held my breath as we crossed over the creek and then sighed good and loud, knowing we were safe and sound at last.

But no. Heck no. That big black Dodge Ram came trucking on over the bridge despite the creek flowing below. What kind of devil was operating that maniac machine?

We were coming up to the intersection of Ashley River and

Parsonage roads, where there's a small mall of shops with a Piggly Wiggly.[3] There would be plenty of lights at last and enough witnesses to maybe help us out. I quick turned right into the parking lot, screeching brakes, and found us a spot to park.

The black Ram came on after us. It swerved into the lot and nearly took off our backside before we pulled out of the way. The truck veered on, finally stopping with a long squeal of the brakes, right in front of the Piggly Wiggly. The truck lights went out, then the engine revved up and quit. It just died.

There was a quiet that I couldn't bear as I sat gripping the steering wheel, staring at that damn Ram. I didn't know what to do. I believe Chuck would have screamed if he had a voice. He unwound himself from his contortion, and we both gazed at that truck. We sat shaking, our nerves idling like a car engine.

Then the driver's door swung open. A lone foot in a pointy black shoe appeared from the darkness of the cab. I only hoped the other foot wasn't cloven like a goat's, or that was Satan for true.

But it wasn't. We watched as a little old lady slowly climbed out of the cab of the Ram. When she stood up, she wasn't more than five feet tall. She shut the door and looked in our general direction, then walked over to us. I glanced at Chuck; he just shrugged. I lowered my window as she approached, because she looked to have a word with us.

"Are you boys all right?" the little old lady asked. "I was afraid you couldn't see me in the dark with your lights off."

"No ma'am, I mean, yes ma'am, we all right," I answered.

"Well, that's good," she said. "You know, I ain't too used to that truck. It's a right fright to drive."

"We're just out for a test drive ourselves, ma'am. I might buy this new car." I was telling her all this but I don't know why I felt like confessing to her. She kind of reminded me of an elderly auntie of mine.

"Do tell," she said. "I may have to be in the market for a new car myself soon."

"How's that, ma'am?" Chuck asked. A true salesman.

"Well, my own car's been actin' up of late. Fact is, it's back to the house, and my son, he's workin' on it. Tryin' to fix it right. He let me barrow his truck to do my grocery shoppin' now. But I tell you, it's a monster to drive."

"Yes ma'am, yes ma'am, I do believe so," I said.

"Well, as long as y'all are all right. I was a little afraid comin' down the road and tryin' to see over that dashboard."

"Yes ma'am, I understand," Chuck interjected, handing her his business card.

"Why, thank you, son. I may have to come visit you," she said to Chuck.

"Yes ma'am." He nodded.

"I'm glad y'all's ok," she said. "All right, now, y'all take care."

"Oh, yes ma'am, that's a plan," I replied.

"Nice to have met you," said Chuck.

We watched her cross to the Piggly Wiggly and go inside to shop. After about a minute, the spell, or whatever it was, wore off, and we began moving as though we were back in real time. Chuck started chuckling. Then, we both laughed out loud till we came near to tears.

I put the car in gear and pulled back out to Ashley River Road. We eased into the traffic and made our way to Savannah Highway and the Ford dealership. It was a welcome sight. Chuck jumped out of the car and came around to my side. I got out and handed him the keys.

"Sold," I told him.

Chuck's face lit up; he was just grinning. "You sure?" he asked me.

"Sure, I'm sure. Less you want to go for another test drive?"

"If it's all the same to you, after our little adventure, I think I'd rather walk. Nothing personal."

"Oh, I understand. But I figure if that car could get me, us, through an experience like we just went through, I ought to honor whatever the Fates mean for things to be. Know what I mean? I believe they're indicating that I should buy this car."

Chuck grabbed my hand and shook and shook it as though he was holding on for dear life. I do believe he wanted a hug, but I think he had already impressed his boss, who was watching through the display window. We went inside to do up all the paperwork.

That night I drove off in my new Ford Taurus, a car with a lot of bull. Now you know how I got it. The car, that is.

The Lowcountry Liar winked at me and said,
"Maybe I should take you for a spin sometime."
"I think you just did!" I replied and laughed.
I for one am glad he is not a car salesman.

Note

This is the Lowcountry Liar's own modern-day variant of Washington Irving's classic tale about the Headless Horseman of Sleepy Hollow. The chase takes place along Ashley River Road, an old highway still well traveled today. He had some fun at the expense of the car salesman, too. It is as true a tale as ever he will tell you.

Chillicothe, Ohio was also the hometown of John Bennett, who transplanted himself in Charleston and became a literary leader for South Carolina during "the Charleston Renaissance" of the 1920s and '30s. He was also a founding member of the South Carolina Poetry Society (1925). Bennett is best known for his novel *Master Skylark* and his collection of Lowcountry conjure tales *The Doctor to the Dead*.

CHAPTER 14

The Little White Dog of White Point Gardens

One fine evening, I was walking along White Point Gardens when I met up with the Lowcountry Liar, who was shrimping from the Ashley River. As the evening blackened into night, he cast this ghost story.

At the southernmost end of the elegant South of Broad Street neighborhood, overlooking the harbor filled by the Ashley and Cooper rivers, lie White Point Gardens, and bubba, you cannot get any farther downtown in residential peninsula Charleston than that. White Point Gardens are so named for all the broken oyster shells discarded by native Indian tribes who fished there ages ago. Wealthy Charlestonians built huge homes upon this old Indian midden, or riverside landfill, as the archaeologists define such a site. It's an impressive achievement, making real estate from available materials. It kind of levels the elite with the street.

Down here, we affectionately call those residents "S.O.B.S.," because they live *S*-outh *o*-f *B*-road *S*-treet. I'll tell you about one of them S.O.B.S., Elizabeth Smith Humphries Hagood. That's a mouthful, I know, but the well-to-do make a claim to prestige by wearing their pedigree on their sleeves. Out of earshot, we commoners called her "Mrs. Shh," because it sounded like a stern command from a strict librarian. The funny thing is, she had retired from the county library downtown, where she'd worked for nearly half a century. She'd also been widowed a while, and her adult children led lives with their families elsewhere.

So, as company Mrs. Shh kept a little white poodle dog as a pet. I don't remember its name. Everywhere Mrs. Shh went, that little white poodle went, too. She'd put the pooch in a little white basket that she carried on her arm. When she went to church service on Sunday, there'd be the poodle in the basket. When she grocery shopped to the Piggly Wiggly, she'd hush up the pup by slipping it a treat, like a Vienna sausage or an Oreo cookie. The stock boys would just smile and shake their heads.

Come nighttime, Mrs. Shh would dine with her canine companion. Lord knows what table scraps made up its supper. Afterwards, she'd snuggle under the bed covers, the little white dog curled up on a throw rug beside the bed. Every night they would watch a television program like "Murder, She Wrote," "Law and Order," or some other syndicated detective show. Mrs. Shh liked mysteries and whodunits. Every night she'd read aloud, for the benefit of her pet pooch as well as herself, just to hear a human voice.

Otherwise, there would be nothing but night sounds and shadows. An occasional Atlantic coast breeze might mysteriously roll in—whistling through the piazzas and open windows as the sunless hours quietly watch the waterfront, the palmetto trees rustling, their big leaves waving like hands. Then Mrs. Shh would slip into slumber like a sigh.

Sometimes when still restless, Mrs. Shh by habit would drop her hand over the side of the bed. Then the little white poodle dog lying on the rug would lick and lick and lick her fingers. It was such a soothing exercise, so soft and sweet, that it soon put Mrs. Shh to sleep. The little white dog proved to be woman's best friend for true.

Some few years ago, on a calm, balmy night like tonight, Mrs. Shh lay in bed. Her sweet pet lay curled up on the rug. Mrs. Shh read the evening paper, this being back in the day when Charleston still had a separate newspaper edition published in late afternoon. She was evermore engrossed in her reading.

One particular story warned that a patient/inmate had taken unauthorized, let alone unsupervised, leave of absence from the state mental institution up in Columbia, the capital. I'm not claiming that the state's capitol building actually *is* the state mental institution. However, the big domed building where the legislature meets, a most notable edifice surrounded by a park full of statues down on State Street, has sometimes been referred to as a loony bin by we the people. Oddly enough, the actual state psych ward *is* a few blocks away, on Bull Street.

Well, the newspaper reported that the patient/inmate had been under guard in a secure cell, undergoing court-ordered observation. He was the sole suspect connected to the questionable disappearances of several elderly ladies. One of them happened to belong to Mrs. Shh's library book club.

The news story gave the escapee's hometown as Charleston. It said he could be anywhere and should be considered dangerous. As she read the news, Mrs. Shh's alarm grew to full-fledged fear.

She put down the paper, picked it up again, reread the headline, and scanned the story for details. The little dog sneezed twice. *Sssshhh! Sssshhh!*

Startled, Mrs. Shh sat bolt upright in bed. She saw nothing sinister, heard nothing strange. She sighed, blessed her dog, and tried to relax again, snuggling under the covers.

The moon was full, but the sky was heavily clouded, so the nightlight flickered off and on almost like a strobe light. Mrs. Shh left on the reading lamp above her headboard, though she had no desire to continue perusing the news. She resolved to sleep, but parts of that scary news story kept poking through her consciousness. She tossed and turned, turned and tossed, restless with worry.

After an age of agonizing minutes, Mrs. Shh decided to enlist the help of her pet. She flipped back the covers, scootched to the side of the bed, and draped her hand over. Sure enough, the little wet tongue began licking and licking. Soon the familiar wet, warm, rhythmic feeling began to soothe her. She began to unwind, really relax.

She was about to drift off to a promising, restful slumber, her constant companion slurping away. She looked through the hazy shadows across the room. A mottled shaft of moonlight shone through the piazza window onto the bedroom floor.

On a throw rug by the window lay her little white poodle dog, curled up, apparently sound asleep. She could hear a soft canine snore. Mrs. Shh frowned.

Then, she screamed.

And fainted.

Something, or someone, was still licking her fingers.

I had handled some shrimp pulled up by the Lowcountry Liar, so my hands were wet and slimy. I sighed slowly. I couldn't say a word.

Note

My wife hates this story and won't let me tell it in her presence. I can't blame her. The elements are found worldwide: a lonely little old lady in the dead of night and a threat from a crazy intruder who doesn't know the meaning of *caveat canum* (beware of the dog). I have heard variants of this tale elsewhere, wherein the intruder kills the dog and leaves a note behind for the widow to discover in the morning, along with her dead pet. That's just plain mean and spiteful. The story is creepy enough without such an unwarranted act.

When South Carolina formally seceded from the Union in 1860, James Louis Petigru, the greatly respected jurist, attorney, and statesman from Charleston who opposed both nullification and secession, made an astute observation about the politics of his day. He said, "South Carolina is too small for a republic, and too large for an insane asylum."

CHAPTER 15

The Long and the Latitude of It

One time I asked the Lowcountry Liar for directions. He told me this Charleston ghost story, as he said, "for good measure."

A ghost story is generally based on circumstantial evidence that can make it somewhat plausible. You debate the details and do the math. Somehow it adds up, sometimes through some kind of eerie arithmetic.

An example is what happened to a state senator's son one summertime years ago. I don't want to mention the surname—I try to protect the innocent, you know—but the family is originally from the Lowcountry and still owns land here, including a tomato farm out to John Island. Well, the senator was a widower, so he spent a lot of his time up at the capitol in Columbia, right in the middle of South Carolina. His only son was about twenty years old and a student at Clemson University, way to the other end of the Lowcountry.

The son was visiting his grandparents out on the family tomato farm. It's off Chisholm Road; I could show you. They had always been an agricultural family, which was the reason why the grandson was studying at Clemson, an agricultural school. I guess he was doing some sort of summer schooling of his own at the family homestead, earning extra credit for extra good works and priming for the future.

One Saturday morning, the young man went up to Cross Seed Store. Every Charlestonian west of the Ashley River knows where the Cross Seed Company building is located. It has been, since forever, a kind of a landmark right there on St. Andrews Boulevard, near the Sycamore Road post office, with Maryville around the corner.[1] But it's said that nothing lasts forever, and today the building houses the West Ashley Pet Clinic. You might say the place has gone from seed to breed or flora to fauna.

Anyway, the young man picked up his list of supplies, paid for them, and headed to his pickup in the parking lot. His arms full of packages, he looked up to see Death, yes, Death itself, down to the corner of Sycamore Road and St. Andrews Boulevard. No mistake, it was a roadside distraction.

Death stared right at the senator's son. There were a good hundred yards between the two. Death raised a shrouded arm and pointed a bony finger at the boy. It twisted its wrist and curled its finger, making a beckoning motion.

The young man stopped cold. He stared at Death a moment. Then he tossed the bags into the back of the truck, spilling everything across the bed. He flung open the driver's door, jumped into the cab, slammed the door, revved the engine, popped the clutch, and peeled out. He quickly got away, crossing four lanes of traffic, miraculously without killing anyone.

He fled to John Island down Savannah Highway, crossing the Lime House Bridge, onto Chisholm Road, and back to the family tomato farm. To his worried grandparents, the terrified grandson related his encounter with Death. They were alarmed that Death singled out the senator's son. They decided all bets were off; this wager wasn't no game. The best bet was for him to go, right then.

So, the young man grabbed his gear, packed his pickup, and hugged and kissed his kin goodbye. He fled the farm, raced up Main Road, and escaped John Island by sailing back over the Lime House Bridge. He would have to fly like the devil's own bat out of hell to elude Death.

After a mile or so, he turned off Savannah Highway to Bee's Ferry Road and followed that on up to Ashley River Road—you have to know your way around the main drags, you know. From there he could take Highway 61 on up to Summerville, twenty miles north, then connect to Interstate 26 and ride that clear into Columbia to his daddy or go on up to Clemson beyond. Of course, he could run down Savannah Highway to Sam Rittenberg Boulevard, Highway 7, and take that up to the interstate. It could be quicker, follow me? Either way, he would soon be safe as stone.

It turns out he turned back towards Charleston, again into West

Ashley. He needed gas and to check the inflation of his tires; he might be on the road for a long haul. One convenient station with a proper air pump not far off the peninsular neck and leading to the interstate happens to be located at a particular crossroads: a local landmark, a real fork in the road.

The owner of the gas station was known as a hardworking, taxpaying, long-suffering, God-fearing Christian who favored flamboyant exaltation of his faith. He displayed selected scriptures on double-sided panels dead set between Highways 171, 61, and 17. At this point on the map, at this particular moment in time, the day's verse read: *But concerning that Day or that Hour, No One Knows. . . . Be on Guard, Stay Awake; Take Heed, Watch*—Mark 13:32–37.

Back at the farm, Grandpa was riled up, just a-fuming and stomping around as if he was putting out a fire. Muttering and cussing, he selected a shotgun from the gun cabinet, pocketed a box of shells, tugged on a ball cap, hugged and kissed his wife, and turned to the front door. He paused at the threshold.

Grandma was worked up too, setting and fretting in her overstuffed rocker, with her pet Chihuahua whimpering in her lap. With shaking hands, she phoned her son the senator up in Columbia. A prerecorded voice told her that her son the senator was out appearing at some grand opening of something or other, and she had to leave a message after the beep. In a shaky voice, she transferred the alarum.

A clap of thunder exploded overhead as Grandpa flung open the front door. The sky looked dark, with a bad overcast of dirty clouds. It looked as though rain would come down in buckets. Grandma, ever a loving wife, got up and fetched her husband's raincoat. She thrust it under his arm.

Down to Cross Seed went Grandpa, but he didn't see hide nor hair of any Grim Reaper. He heard, then spotted, an EMS ambulance and several police cars tearing down St. Andrews Boulevard. Grandpa got a feeling as bad as the oncoming thunderstorm overhead. Down the road he chased the EMS to the fork of Highways 171, 61, and 17. It was all there on the signs.

There at the intersection Grandpa saw what caused the hullabaloo—an auto accident. A fire truck was angled on the shoulder of Ashley River Road, and hoses crisscrossed Old Town Road. The intersection was washed down all around the wreck. A haze of smoke lifted above, and the smell of gasoline and burnt tires lingered in the air. Grandpa passed the police and paramedics, growing more worried, then stopped when he saw the make and model of the mangled machine in the road. It looked like his grandson's pickup truck. The medics had already covered a body.

Then he saw it. Next to a grove of pine trees at the sharpest bend in the road, apart from everybody else, stood Death itself. Grandpa parked and clambered out of his truck, hiding the shotgun under his raincoat. His sciatica was tailor-made for limping legit with a loaded firearm down his leg.

Making his way past the concerned crowd and evermore gripping that gun, Grandpa stalked Death. He marched right up to the Grim Reaper and stared him dead in the eye.

"Why you scaring the living daylights outta my grandson like that?" he cried. "Why, I oughta fill your godless carcass with a backside full of buckshot! Have a taste of these double barrels—"

"No need for that, sir," said Death politely, raising an arm. Grandpa's shotgun followed in an upwards swing as if magnetized but did not fire. Slowly, Death lowered its arm; Grandpa's weapon followed till it was pointing at the ground.

"But you nearly scared the life outta my grandson!" he protested.

"Yes sir," said Death. "Sorry for such an errant appearance. I can assure you, sir, that your grandson took me quite by surprise, too. I never expected to meet him so soon. You see, I already had an appointment with him, later today, at this intersection."

"Que sera, sera, anyone?" I asked and shrugged.
"That's the point," said the Lowcountry Liar.

Note

This is an ancient tale told worldwide. The oldest known variant comes from the sands of Mesopotamia. The timeless message stays the same, though. You can beat your gums, you can beat a drum, and at poker maybe you can beat an inside straight, but you cannot beat your fate.

CHAPTER 16

She Loves Me Knot

> *Matrimony is a special bond encompassing love, trust, dedication, and endurance. As proof, the Lowcountry Liar proposed this ghost story of love at first sight and last sight, too.*

Ashley loved Cooper. Cooper loved Ashley. They shared a love as strong as the ever-lasting flow of the Ashley and Cooper rivers running along the east and west sides of peninsular Charleston.[1] Like their namesake rivers, Ashley and Cooper met here in Charleston. We like to say the two bodies of water meet at the harbor to form the Atlantic Ocean—just a little local geographic joke. Ashley and Cooper's love for each other ran as deep and vast as an ocean.

Back in the days of colonial Carolina, Charleston was the crown jewel of England's North American empire. The ancestral families of Ashley and Cooper came separately to settle in the Lowcountry. They each established plantations, built businesses and homes, and founded family lineages.

Ashley's family had arrived in England much earlier, a few years before the dawn of the eighteenth century. They had emigrated from France to escape the royal persecution of Protestants, the Huguenots—think Presbyterians with a French accent. Aptly enough, Ashley's family name happened to be Hazard. Her refugee family clung together and generally only socialized with other Huguenots while in England. When they later immigrated to British North America, the Hazard clan kept together as a colony within a colony. They were right secretive folk, the Hazards. What they were so secretive about was anyone's guess.

Cooper's family for generations had been barrel makers, so, like the Smiths, Carpenters, Masons, and others, the occupation became the surname. See, when you make a barrel, what's inside gets *cooped* up. Cooper's first name actually was Adam, but as a boy, he loved to climb inside one of the many barrels at the family's factory and play hide and seek, so his pet name became "Cooper" too. Back then, everyone needed barrels, the commonest containers for everything, the Tupperware of the times. Cooper's family came to the Carolina colony to capitalize on Charleston's obvious demand for barrels.

One day in town, Ashley and Cooper met. It was love at first sight, for true. She saw a handsome, enterprising young man. He saw the most beautiful, elegant, enticing woman ever to cross his path. They spoke briefly, shyly, and began courting.

Soon Ashley and Cooper became inseparable, seen together all over Charleston. Tall, redheaded Cooper stood out in a crowd, easily recognizable. Pretty little Ashley turned heads by always wearing a silk scarf wrapped around her neck. Whatever the occasion, her attire always included a scarf of vibrant color to accent her ensemble. Some folks thought it vain; others thought it quaint, like a cultural trait. Cooper looked forward to seeing what color she'd pick next for her neckwear. Ashley liked to keep him guessing. Sometimes he would try to untie her scarf, but she always kept him at arm's length. She was ever a chaste lady.

After a suitable courtship, he proposed marriage. At the wedding, she wore a gorgeous gown of white with a high collar and a delicate veil over her head. Wrapped round her throat was a wide white ribbon of Carolina silk.[2] It fairly shone, it was so bright.

At last, Cooper would know Ashley completely. Or so he thought. Even on their wedding night, Ashley wore a wrap around her neck to sleep in. Cooper realized with shock that her air of mystery might hide a phobia. He told her his fear that she would choke, but she assured him that she had practiced the habit since she had been a little girl. An odd family custom, Cooper assumed. Every night thereafter, Ashley wore a wrap to bed, as she did during the day.

They were a sweet couple, setting up house together and starting a new life partnership. A year later, they were blessed with the first of four children. Ashley ran the household, overseeing her brood. Cooper continued cooping, keeping the family barrel business in business.

Still, Cooper's curiosity called to him. Some nights he would stay awake, waiting for Ashley to drift off to sleep so he could untie her scarf. Yet he never could keep awake much longer than she would. He finally determined that he would never be able to loosen the knot, let alone unwrap the scarf, without rousing her.

When Ashley bathed or dressed, Cooper hung around hoping to catch her unawares. She had to expose her throat at some time, but still Cooper never saw Ashley's naked neck. In time, Cooper resigned himself to loving Ashley with all her imperfections. He loved her for all he was worth, for all she was worth, and she reciprocated. His curiosity about her scarves passed as time passed, surpassed by the security of their love.

Over many years, Ashley and Cooper marked anniversaries and birthdays and finally celebrated their children's weddings. Just as the family expanded, the family business expanded along with the shipping trade between the colonies and mother country. After a while, though, irreconcilable differences brought on the American Revolution and the ultimate divorce from royal sovereignty.

Ashley, Cooper, and the whole family survived the turmoil. After independence, the family carried on. The booming barrel business kept the clan well financed, well into the future.

Not long after the new congress ratified the Constitution, Ashley's ever-healthy constitution began failing her.[3] When she had to take to bed, Cooper kept right at her side, day and night. The family, growing concerned for Ashley's health, soon grew concerned for Cooper's welfare as well. His stamina was tested by his everlasting, steadfast affection for the love of his life. After so many years, fears, and tears, Ashley and Cooper still had each other. Ashley still wore a scarf around her neck. Cooper by now had fulfilled his fealty by buying her a new scarf for every wedding anniversary.

They had shared so much, living a long full life together, and they would share the end, too. They had no secrets to reveal, except for the secret of Ashley's scarves, which Cooper had accepted. That mystery was still hanging on.

Poor, debilitated Ashley couldn't hang on and succumbed to fate. Cooper, at her side to the last, now became disconsolate, desperately disbelieving the finality. Bereaved, he bent over Ashley. His tears fell upon her face, upon her scarf. Cooper stared at her, at the scarf.

Without another thought, he began to untie the scarf. He would now at last know, before he died, how she looked with a naked neck. He unwound the scarf, round and round, till the last wrapping was left. Carefully, tenderly, Cooper unwound the last of the scarf from Ashley's neck . . . and . . .

Her head fell off!

Before I could stop him, the Lowcountry Liar added, "Ain't that a barrel of laughs?"

Note

Here is another old chestnut found throughout the country, wrapped up with a bow, or for a beau.

CHAPTER 17

Who's Up First?

Baseball has been called America's favorite pastime, followed by swapping stories about the game. The Lowcountry Liar told me this sporty little tale as, he said, "a full account of no foul play."

Hank and Aaron were the best of boyhood friends. They grew up together in rural Dorchester County near Summerville and learned early on what a hard day of work really is. Their favorite pastime was playing baseball. They would play till dark if they could, sometimes later than that, all the better to improve with practice.

They played pickup games in sandlots with other local boys, moved on to official little-league teams, and kept up their athletic skills all through high school. Both boys played all-star games and pennant playoffs and won a slew of trophies. In college, they played for the Carolina Gamecocks on full scholarships, and from there they graduated through the farm system right into the major leagues.

It was more difficult to stay together as teammates after that. Players came and went from team to team in managerial deals or rotated to and from the minors. Other players left because of injuries or to pursue new interests. Hank and Aaron hung on, playing what might not be called the sport of kings but definitely the sport of the king's men. Baseball was their whole lives.

As a pitcher, Hank threw strikes using a crazy knuckleball, serious screwball, or sneaky slider. He put up very respectable stats against scores of batters. As a shortstop, Aaron practically had a net for a glove—nothing got past him into the outfield, and he turned dozens of double plays. He could also swing a bat and had an enviable record of RBIs. Both men had long impressive careers as professional baseball players; both were profiled on several issues of collectible cards. They each had a World Series championship ring, though for different teams in different years.

After several seasons, Hank and Aaron reached the age and the conclusion that they were ready to hang up the cleats and oil the gloves for the last time. They retired from major-league baseball and returned to their hometown roots. Still, the game was in their blood; they continued in it with new careers coaching local ball teams, racking up more impressive stats every year.

After several seasons more, Hank and Aaron finally, permanently, benched themselves on Hank's front porch, riding rockers and reminiscing about great plays and great players. They reminded one another of any number of fabulous homerun hits, dramatic near-impossible catches, historic hit and runs, or squeeze plays at home plate. They would recite their own stats of RBIs and ERAs to others who stopped by to chat.

As the years passed by like extra innings, Hank and Aaron became concerned more and more with when they might dress out for the final, mortal game. They got to speculating as to whether or not baseball was played up in heaven. They made a pact that whichever of them got to heaven first would find out and let the other know, too.

As fate would have it, like the famous "Casey at the Bat," Aaron the shortstop struck out first; he passed away peacefully in his sleep one night. Hank the pitcher was left to sit alone on his porch, pondering about playing baseball in heaven. Then, about a week after Aaron's funeral, Hank looked up to see his old teammate coming up the walk, his figure a little faded.

"Aaron?" Hank asked. "Is that you?"

"Yeah, Hank, it's me," Aaron answered, "though not exactly 'in the flesh,' you see."

"Heh, heh, no, but you look 'in the pink,' considering."

"I suppose so. Listen here, Hank, I've come back to give you the news."

"You mean about playing baseball up in heaven?"

"Yeah, that's right. Only, I got good news and bad news."

"Better give me the good news first, Bubba."

"Ok. The good news is that, sure enough, they play baseball in heaven!"

"Hallelujah! I just knew it! That's great news to hear, Aaron."

"Yep, they got leagues of their own, and there ain't no such thing as extra innings!"

"That's great, Aaron."

"But there's the bad news, too."

"So, what else you got to tell me, friend?"

"Well, the bad news is, Hank, you're scheduled to pitch tomorrow!"

"You're outta there!" I cried. The Lowcountry Liar didn't balk at that.

Note

This is one of those jokes that you don't want to be the butt of. But then again, you can't beat your fate. This is a favorite that the Lowcountry Liar tells, especially during baseball season. Maybe it makes you wonder about the real value of the MVP award. Batter up!

Notes

Chapter 1

1. The 1925 novel *Porgy* was written by DuBose Heyward (1885-1940) of Charleston. He later collaborated with George (1898-1937) and Ira (1890-1983) Gershwin to develop the story into the first American opera, *Porgy and Bess* (1935).

Chapter 2

1. The Confederates had five forts guarding the channel and harbor of Charleston: Fort Sumter at the harbor's mouth across from Fort Moultrie on Sullivan's Island, Forts Wagner and Gregg on Morris Island along the channel, and Fort Johnson on James Island just inside the harbor on the Ashley River. The forts had overlapping "rings of fire," and the Confederates kept the blockading Union fleet out of the port.

2. One of my old Charleston addresses was #3-B Zig Zag Alley.

3. Secessionville, South Carolina, on James Island south of Charleston, was where the Confederates defended against a superior Union assault on June 16, 1862. It was the first land combat in the area and resulted in a Confederate victory.

Chapter 3

1. The Battle of Shiloh took place on April 6-7, 1862. U. S. Grant defeated Albert Sidney Johnston (may he rest in peace).

Chapter 4

1. Winnsboro, county seat of Fairfield County, South Carolina and referred to as the "Charleston of the Upcountry," was cofounded by the Winn brothers in 1785. My family settled there in 1772.

2. Charles, Lord Cornwallis—the British general who capitulated to George Washington at Yorktown, Virginia, the last major siege of the Revolution—is credited with naming Fairfield County for its "fair fields," when he visited the area in 1780. At the time, Cornwallis was campaigning against the rebels, led by the likes of Thomas Sumter (the Fighting Gamecock), Francis Marion (the Swamp Fox), and Nathaniel Greene (the Fighting Quaker). The McCréight family served under both Sumter and Marion (and thus under Greene). During the winter in Winnsboro of 1780-81, some McCréights also served as "captive hosts" to Lord Cornwallis (then ill with perhaps malaria) and his redcoats when they regrouped for the season. That "visit" is a story for another time.

3. Robert Mills (August 12, 1781-March 3, 1855) is known as America's first native-born and native-trained architect. Among his many works, he designed practically every county courthouse in South Carolina, as well as the Washington Monument obelisk and several federal buildings in our nation's capital.

4. The "McCréight House," as it has become known, still stands intact, chimneys included, on Van Der Horst Street in Winnsboro, just a block from the main market

square. We built the house in 1774, using only wood joints and wood pegs to lock it all together. It is reputed to be the oldest such structure still standing in the state of South Carolina. It is unique and part of the historic district of Winnsboro. Go see.

5. Donegal is the westernmost county of old Ulster province in the north of Ireland, whence my family emigrated to America in 1772. Clare is a western county of Connaught province in western Ireland, where ancient McCréights pursued useful occupations, among them storytelling.

Chapter 5

1. Lord Edward Fitzgerald (1763-98) was an Irish revolutionary.

2. The United Irishmen (ca. 1793-98) were part of a revolutionary political movement inspired by both the American and French revolutions.

3. Wolfe Tone (1763–98) was an Irish revolutionary.

4. Robert Emmet (1778-1803) was an Irish nationalist and Republican who led an unsuccessful uprising. He was executed for his trouble and is an Irish national hero.

5. John Caldwell Calhoun (1780-1850) wrote "the Nullification Papers," arguing that the Ninth and Tenth amendments, recognizing each state as a separate, sovereign, free, and independent entity, give each state the right to nullify Federal law should it prove onerous to the state.

6. The Battle of Antietam, known as the Battle of Sharpsburg in the South, occurred on September 17, 1862, and is the bloodiest single-day battle in U.S. history.

Chapter 6

1. The Legare family is not at all to be associated with the fictional Simon Legree, the transplanted villain of *Uncle Tom's Cabin*, by Harriet Beecher Stowe.

2. The word *aëdes*, for mosquito, comes from the Greek language meaning "unpleasant," or specifically, "not sweet." This species of pest can give you the deadly yellow fever, which is not at all pleasant or sweet. Yellow fever was also referred to as "the black vomit." The fever affects internal organs galore, such that no matter your appetite, you cannot even keep down sipping water. The body shuts down and coma ensues; too often death is the cure. Medicine in the nineteenth century wasn't nearly as available nor sophisticated as healthcare is now.

3. Buried beneath the Lowcountry lies the Woodstock Fault, which makes the area susceptible to earthquakes. The biggest earthquake ever east of the Mississippi, estimated at about 7.5 on the Richter scale, occurred at Charleston on August 31, 1886. Many buildings in downtown Charleston today have iron "earthquake rods" emplaced to stabilize the structures. You can distinguish these buildings by the iron washers decorating their walls. Besides the earthquakes, there have been horrendous hurricanes, terrible tornadoes, fantastic fires and floods—practically every natural disaster except a flow of volcanic lava. That's all in addition to the countless deadly epidemics, sometimes simultaneous, of smallpox, malaria, yellow fever, and other diseases brought by boat to this city by the sea. It's all part of the charm of Charleston.

Charlestonians also have suffered several manmade fiascos, such as marauding pirates, Indian and slave uprisings, enemy bombardments—foreign and domestic—as well as the invasion and occupation. Blackbeard blockaded our harbor, and the British Army and Navy occupied the city for a while, as did the Federal Army and Navy during Reconstruction. Despite it all, to spite them all, we are still here.

4. The marble mausoleum of the Legare/Legree family can be visited at the back of the graveyard by the Edisto Island Presbyterian Church. You can see the little stone house from the only road, Highway 174. There is no door to the vault to this day. The incident at the end of this story, when the stranger asks about the door-less crypt, actually happened to me and another storyteller friend of mine (Matt Fletcher, from Winnsboro).

We had stopped by the church after telling stories at a program at the Edisto branch of the county library. We were standing in the graveyard and I had just finished telling this tale to Matt. We both sensed an eerie feeling, even though it was a cloudless July afternoon. When that other fellow showed up and asked that question, we were truly spooked by the uncanny coincidence.

Chapter 7
1. *The Code of Honor* (1838, second edition 1858) was compiled by former South Carolina governor and Charleston minister John Lyde Wilson. It outlined the official conduct required to challenge and shoot an opponent who had allegedly besmirched your honor. The practice had been common since colonial days, especially influenced by our French immigrants.

2. There are many variant spellings of the name MacRaith, meaning son of ("mac") grace, luck, prosperity, and fortune. Other spellings start with either Mc or Mac and end in Rea, Crea, Rae, Crae, Ray, Cray, Rath, or Grath. There is even Magraw. Creighton is an Anglicized spelling. McCréight is apparently a somewhat Anglicized Scots-Irish spelling.

So, rather obliquely, I am related to Judge Andrew Gordon McGrath. More ironic, I have a brother named Andrew whose son's middle name is Gordon—coincidence?

Furthermore, the clan McGrath/MacRea has more than one close-call connection to civil combat in South Carolina. There is the September 29, 1856, duel between Edward Magrath/McGrath and *Charleston Mercury* editor William Taber, who published alleged slander against his brother Judge Andrew Gordon. The judge was then a candidate for Congress. The result was that on the third round of shots, after one last debate, Taber fell dead. His coeditor, John Heart, and the editorialist Edmund Rhett, Jr., both pledged to continue the duel, but satisfaction had been met.

The hits just keep on coming. In 1906, shortly after Dr. Thomas Ballard McDow died during the summer of 1904, his younger brother Edgar S. "Arthur" McDow, back in homestead Lancaster, shot a man in a dispute over a bill for late merchandise. He was convicted of assault and fined, then a few months later was shotgunned dead himself by his brother-in-law in yet another argument. He finally died of his wounds on November 12, 1906, seventeen years and eight months to the day of the killing of Captain Dawson.

More oddly enough, in March 1907—the eighteenth anniversary of Dawson's death—came the trial of Dr. E. S. McDow's killer. The fellow who shot and killed him in Lancaster was named John A. Bridges. Bridges was acquitted in fifteen minutes.

Again, this is an interesting connection to a bridge and dueling, referring back to the DuBois Bridge and the infamous Cash-Shannon Duel. Also ironic, TB McDow slays Dawson in March and is acquitted the following November, while his younger brother is slain in November and his killer acquitted the following March. What goes around . . .

So go some strange, roundabout connections in time. Researching this story, I was amazed at the associations among Judge Andrew Gordon McGrath, Attorney William McCréight Shannon, Charleston, Camden, Lancaster, DuBois bridge and town, and dueling in South Carolina. What are the odds? A one-in-a-million shot?

3. Carolina Day commemorates the first total victory for independence in the American colonies during the Revolutionary War. Fort Sullivan on Sullivan's Island, built of hastily constructed sand dunes at a bevel angle covered with palmetto-tree logs and manned by a few hundred Carolina militia with fewer than three dozen cannons, for half a day beat back a British fleet of nine warships having nearly three hundred cannons. We suffered only a dozen dead and four dozen wounded. The British had hundreds of casualties, lost a ship, and would not attack South Carolina again for nearly four years. Less

than a week later, somewhat inspired by the events at Charleston harbor, the Declaration of Independence was proclaimed.

Chapter 8
1. Towns such as Williamsport, Maryland; Staunton and Roanoke, Virginia; Salisbury, North Carolina; and Camden, South Carolina came into existence along the Southern migratory route of the Scots-Irish pioneers. The path was known as the "Great Pennsylvania Wagon Road," and in South Carolina it followed an old Catawba Indian path, which is now U.S. Highway 521 through Lancaster, Kershaw, and Sumter counties.
2. Copper canteens were common during the colonial era.

Chapter 9
1. Alston and Manigault are very old Charleston surnames. Beauregard refers to Confederate general Pierre Gustave Toutant Beauregard, the "Protector of Charleston."

Chapter 10
1. Frank Howard Field at Memorial Stadium, Clemson University, is commonly known as "Death Valley."

Chapter 12
1. Boiled peanuts and benne-seed wafers are Lowcountry delicacies. Benne is sesame. Be sure to check out the Charleston Market.
2. Hampton Park, adjacent to the Citadel on peninsular Charleston, is named for the venerable Wade Hampton, South Carolina governor, U.S. senator, and Confederate lieutenant general who commanded Lee's cavalry. The park was originally the Charleston Race Course—horseracing was a big business in the state, and the Hamptons led the Lowcountry in the horse business.

Chapter 13
1. *Coota* is the name of the Lowcountry Liar's houseboat. A cooter is a local turtle.
2. Wappoo is an area west of the Ashley River along Wappoo Creek.
3. Piggly Wiggly is a supermarket chain in the South and Midwest, founded in 1916 in Memphis, Tennessee. We're Big on the Pig.

Chapter 15
1. St. Andrews Boulevard splits northeast at Old Town Road (Highway 171) and northwest at Ashley River Road (Highway 61), which also leads southwards to Savannah Highway (Highway 17).

Chapter 16
1. The Ashley and Cooper rivers are the lateral waterways of peninsular Charleston. They were named in honor of the leading lord proprietor who established the colony—Lord Anthony Ashley Cooper, a close friend of King Charles II, for whom Charleston was named.
2. A silk trade was begun by Huguenots in the Lowcountry during the colonial period, but the expense of time, space, and upkeep of the delicate silkworms made for a less than profitable venture, and it was discontinued.
3. The United States Constitution was fully ratified in 1790. South Carolina was the eighth state to ratify it, on May 23, 1788.

Glossary

How y'all? Welcome to the South Carolina Lowcountry, a place where euphemisms, solecisms, and diphthongs hang in the air like the Spanish moss dripping from the live oak trees. Here you will find translations of the local lingo that was used in these stories. Some historical notes are included as well.

amadán. Irish Gaelic for fool, idiot.
Bat-tree. The High Battery down at White Point Gardens is the old seawall on the Cooper River, protecting the east side of Charleston. A battery is something you put in a flashlight.
Bergère hat. "Shepherdess" hat that provided protection from sunburn during outdoor work.
boo hag. A Lowcountry variant of the dreaded vampire.
boyos. Irish slang for guys, mates, pals, buddies, bros, bubbas, etc.
bubba. Brother.
bucko. See *boyo*.
bummers. Yankee soldiers (thieves) who would steal property and valuables at any cost, including murder (also known as "stab and grab" duty).
cabinetmaker. An all-purpose carpenter.
conjure. Root; the hex-heavy, mojo-stirring belief system of the Gullah Lowcountry.
Coopa Riva. The Cooper River, on the east side of Charleston.
Divil. Irish slang for the Devil.
eejit. Irish slang for idiot.
folly. Foolish, or a useless structure. In this book, a maritime meaning applies: from a distance offshore, the land appears to be mainland but upon closer inspection proves to be merely an island, and it would be folly to land there. An example is Folly Island, outside Charleston harbor.
fufteen. Fifteen.
fushing. Fishing.
haint. A haunt, ghost, spirit, bump-in-the-night type.
haints, boo hags, plat eyes. A combination of heebie-jeebies, real and imagined.
hinky. Out of the ordinary.
Holy City. Charleston's nickname. It comes from the traditional exercise of religious tolerance here, epitomized by the many houses of worship representing the diverse denominations of divinity. It's debatable whether there are more churches or restaurants in the city. Either way, it is all nourishment for the body and the soul.
Is maith sin. Irish Gaelic for "It's good," "It's a good thing." This expression has been borrowed and bent into English as an enthusiastic adjective, "smashing!"
Jaysus. Irish slang for Jesus.
kee-yarn. A "locophone," a crazy local word made up from "killed" and "carrion." You'll know that odor when you smell it.

Manigault. Pronounced as if a fast car races by and you say, "Man, he go!" It is a surname brought to the Lowcountry by early Huguenot immigrants.
mash. To press, as in "mash the elevator button."
miasma. Poisonous vapor believed to cause malaria, supposedly released by exposed carcasses.
midden. A prehistoric human trash dump of bones, shells, utensils, etc.
mojo. Medicine of the conjure kind.
mumbly peg. A knife-tossing game of both skill and chance, favored by ambling-rambling-gambling boys but dreaded by their mothers.
och. Irish Gaelic for oh.
piazza. A wide, building-long porch, roomy enough for strolling. It comes from the Italian for a roofed walkway. If you can play shuffleboard on it, it's a piazza; you play checkers on a porch. Haint blue is a common color for the ceiling.
plat eyes. Flat, wide, saucerlike eyes of night critters stalking about—a special kind of haint. Often met on rural roads, plat eyes will chase you to death, truly, unless you can cross flowing water, which they cannot.
pluff mud. Unique Lowcountry mud, with a particularly pungent, but harmless, sulfurous odor. Think of burning bacon, fresh-roasted coffee, and a smoking cigar.
poteen. Homebrewed whiskey (Irish Gaelic for the Water of Life), aka white lightning.
Prioleau. Pronounced "Pray-low." It is a surname brought to the Lowcountry by early Huguenot immigrants.
pure-tee. Purely, completely, wholly.
rice bed. A particular piece of Lowcountry furniture that is raised about two feet off the floor. This is necessary for cool ventilation during the summer, but with clearance for winter braziers to warm from below.
rye-cheer. Right here.
scalawag and carpetbagger. A scalawag is a Southerner who colluded with Northern occupiers, and a carpetbagger is a Northern "businessman" who arrived in the South during the occupation to take advantage of the spoils of war.
shrumping. Shrimping.
single house. Unique Lowcountry home structure. Traditionally two stories high, it is one room wide and two rooms long, with a central staircase and a piazza.
sláinte! Irish Gaelic for "to health!" (a toast).
suh. Sir.
youse. You, as the Yankee equivalent of the Southern y'all. It was borrowed from mostly Irish immigrants coming into the northeastern United States.